TOP HEAVY

TOP HEAVY

RHONDA DeCHAMBEAU

Holiday House · New York

Copyright © 2025 by Rhonda DeChambeau

All Rights Reserved

HOLIDAY HOUSE is registered in the U.S. Patent and Trademark Office.

Printed and bound in April 2025 at Sheridan, Chelsea, MI, USA.

www.holidayhouse.com

First Edition

1 3 5 7 9 10 8 6 4 2

Library of Congress Cataloging-in-Publication Data is available.

ISBN: 978-0-8234-5813-4 (hardcover)

EU Authorized Representative: HackettFlynn Ltd, 36 Cloch Choirneal, Balrothery, Co.
Dublin, K32 C942, Ireland. EU@walkerpublishinggroup.com

For Chris and Donna and Colin

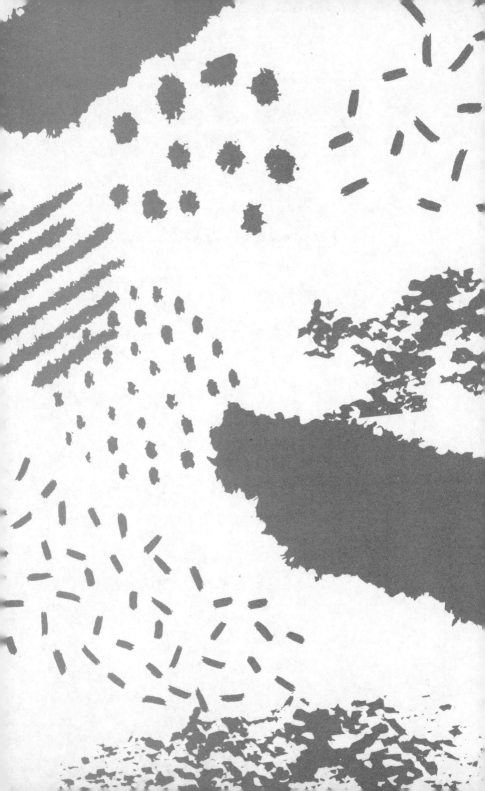

SOARING

When I dance
I grow wings.

In the studio
      I am soaring—
              energy pulsing
                    adrenaline pouring—
                          Finding my freedom
                                the music roaring.

I hear bass notes through the balls of my feet.
Every beat
syncs to the thing
alive in my chest.

      Heart   HEART
      Heart   HEART
      Heart   HEART

The studio mirror
catches glimpses of me
whipping around
twirling
spinning.

The beat powers muscle and bone.
      Rhythm radiates through me.
            Arms   out to fingertips.
            Legs   out to toes.
Lifting
      S t r e t c h i n g.

      Until I am
          flying.
SOARING

COMING DOWN

Mia's eyes follow me
                in the mirror.

We are happiest here.
Just the two of us.
Working.
Playing.
Creating.

I pirouette
        chassé
                grand jeté.

Each name as beautiful
as the movement itself.

And when I soar, mid-air,
there is the
        upswing
and a heavy
        downswing,
an ache in the sides of my neck
and across my back
and the straps of two sports bras
saw into my shoulders.

At my sternum,
my double D's thump in unison.

Top heavy
is what Miss Regina says.

It makes me think of
capsizing
      under the weight
      of my own chest.

Then coming down,
stumble.
      Off kilter
          Off balance
              Just off.

I'm not soaring,
so much as reaching
      for something that seems
          to be
          farther
          and
          farther
          away.

UNFINISHED

Because there isn't enough room
anywhere else in our house,
I practice in the basement.

The basement is
unfinished,
which means
it's just open space with
concrete walls and floors
and pipes running overhead.

After I earned
my spot on the Junior team,
Dad installed a barre
on the bare wooden studs
next to the stairs.
Behind that, the big mirror
he bought used
when the Kmart went out of business.

I gave up
tap and ballet
(for the two obvious
reasons on my chest)
and focus on
contemporary and lyrical.
I can't really do floorwork
on the concrete,

so I focus on my technique,
my turns, my flexibility.

The basement gets cold
in the winter.

It's always dusty,
and the concrete
knocks hard against my feet and my knees.
But I'm down here every night
training and working and hoping.

Mia and I have dreams
of making the Elite team,
the highest level of competition at our studio.
We should hear any day.
Miss Regina announces the new Elite team
at the end of summer
before the new season starts.

For now,
the music from my little speaker
echoes against the cement walls.
The water heater and
Mom's old exercise bike
cheer me on silently.

Pieces of me
flash in the mirror:
pointed toes
strong arms
graceful fingertips
and
my boobs
bobbing
in their double-sports-bra

I keep going, until
I hear the door creak
at the top of the stairs.

Esme? Mom calls.
That's enough now.
Your dad's trying to rest.

I click off my speaker
and put in my earbuds
instead.

For me,
there's still so much
work to be done.
No time
for rest. I am
unfinished, too.

WHAT IT MEANS TO BE ELITE

When the sweat soaks through
my leotard
or runs in rivulets
down my back

When the muscles in my legs burn
quads on fire
hamstrings spark and twinge

When pain sends a needle through
my neck, a burning thread
through my torso each time I turn
When my shoulders strain
against the weight of my chest

I think of what it means
to be Elite.

How my world would change
if I were Elite.

I would leap   higher.
Hold my head   higher.

Somehow
my chest
would matter less.

At the end of last season
after the final competition
Miss Regina said to us,
me and Mia,
Keep it up, girls.
You may just have a shot at Elite next year.

My heart lifted,
holding tight
to the string carrying those
helium words.

I know
my world would change
if I were Elite.

THIS IS IT

Once a week
even in summer,
Mia and I help teach the little kids.

They scuttle over the floor
like hermit crabs
in leotards and tutus.
And Miss Regina needs help
keeping all eyes on her.
Choreography for hermit crabs
is no easy task.

This is the last week of
Summer Session
and the studio—
the kids
Mia
Me
all of us—
are filled with the nervous energy
        that comes with
                endings and beginnings.

At the end of class,
Miss Regina calls,
Esme. Mia.
Come here please.

Mia and I lock eyes.
This is it!

The little girls trot toward the door,
toward the parents
on the other side
of the one-way window.

Mia laces her fingers through mine.

I feel her
breathe
in.

The hard work of our summer,
long days in the upstairs studio,
have left a mark.

Her knee is perpetually wrapped,
and my shoulders have started to scab
from where my bra straps dug in.
But damn if we're not good.

Really good.

The best ones, by far,
on the Junior team.

I know you two have worked really hard,
Miss Regina begins to say,
and my heart hardens
because this does not sound like
congratulations.

She tells us how she's noticed
our hours of practice time.
Above and beyond.
We've decided,
you are ready for
Elite.
Both of you.

10

CELEBRATION

Mia and I squeal
and jump
and hug
and Mia starts to cry.

Miss Regina grants us
a rare smile
when she finally says,
Congratulations, girls.

Mia and I will be the youngest on the team,
but Miss Regina tells us not to worry,
she wouldn't have selected us
unless we were ready.

It will be a lot of work,
Miss Regina warns.
*Classes are Tuesday and Thursday evenings
and Saturday mornings
in addition to work
you put in on your own.*

In response,
Mia and I
jump
        up
                and
                        down.
Her on her bad knee
        and me with
                my boobs
                      bouncing.
Like neither thing matters.
Like we are still five
instead of fifteen.

CONGRATULATIONS

Mom picks me up
on her way home from work.

When I tell her the news,
she hugs me
from the driver's seat.

Esme, that's amazing.
I'm so proud of you.
Her eyes glisten.

When I get home
Dad's in the place
                he's been for the last three weeks.

In the recliner
that we borrowed from
Uncle Larry,
who isn't really my uncle,
but one of Dad's oldest friends.

The chair is plaid and smells like dog,
but it is the only way
Dad is   almost   comfortable.

He is awake.
Hey, Pumpkin.

Dad, guess what?
We made Elite! Me and Mia!
Both of us!

That's really something.
You should be proud,
Dad says. *Congratulations.*

I lean in and let him put his
slow arms around me.

We've recently perfected this
twisty, sideways
kind of hug, one
             where my head leans against his cheek
                      for the   beat   of a second.

I do it now,
the top of my hair tangling
in the unshaved forest of his cheek
as I pull away.

Just be sure you're keeping your grades up, right?
Dad says, trying to sit up more.

He cringes   sucks in   a big   breath
and tries to smile at me
             through gritted teeth.

Yes, Dad.

Grades first.

I know, I say.

I lean in and peck his cheek,
try to ignore the stubble
that's already turning into a beard,
and the greasiness of his hair,
the faint stink of BO
mixed with the dog chair.

Love you, Pumpkin, he calls.

Love you, too, Dad.

CONVERSATION I OVERHEAR #1

Before I close my door
I overhear

How much is the Elite team going to cost?
Dad's voice, followed by
a deep inhale.

Mom answers
with a sigh so small
I barely hear it.
What can we do?
It's what she loves.

Yeah, but if we don't have the money,
we don't have it.

We'll find a way. We always do, Mom says.

Things are different now.
Then Dad's voice, out of breath,
     like he's been climbing stairs
          instead of readjusting a damaged spine
              in a threadbare recliner,
                all the stuffing wearing thin.
Will it . . . get her . . . a scholarship . . . for college?

Maybe.

Silence.

THE PHILOSOPHY OF DAD

Education, he always says,
is the only thing that matters.

I wish, he always says,
that I knew that
when I was in high school.

When I was little,
he called himself a bug guy,
                back when he was proud.

I know he thinks that maybe
with an education
he wouldn't have ended up
like this.

It's the difference between him
and Mia's dad   who is a dentist,
or our neighbor—Mr. Miller—who works on computers.

Maybe then
Dad wouldn't have gone into
the old house on the West Side,
the one built in the 1800s
with stairs just as old
leading down
to a basement
with a mice infestation.

The third step
        from the top
                giving way
                        under his steel-toed work boots

15

sending him
crashing

through splintered wood

landing on the broken furnace
left under the stairs to rust.

The old lady,
not quite as old as the house,
but almost,
so slow to hear his screams.

So slow
dialing 911
while Dad waited

his body twisted on the broken scraps of metal
and shards of rotted wood.

Waiting for the ambulance,
his spine on fire,
wishing he'd gotten an education,
so he could have worked on
someone's teeth
or their computer
instead of this.

PARTNERS WE DON'T CHOOSE

This year, I have
Chemistry fourth period,
and my lab partner, Celine,
     is afraid of the Bunsen burner.

Through the plastic lenses of our goggles,
         we peer out at one another,
           creatures from different worlds.

She is a senior,
and though
I'm two years behind her
I catch things faster,
grabbing onto the jumble of letters
that Mr. Silva tosses out,
the ones marching
into their boxes
on the Periodic Table.

My brain is quicker,
but my body is thicker
than Celine's,
whose bony wrists look
like they might snap
holding the glass beaker.

On our second day, she looks
down at her own English tea cups,
and says
They must get heavy, huh?

        I don't answer.

I just think
more than a handful
is a waste.

A waste, I wonder,
of what?
        Of flesh?
            Of meat?
                  Of muscle?
                    Of me?

I light the Bunsen burner,
hiding my red-hot cheeks
        behind the blue flame.

THOSE WE CHOOSE

She said that?
Mia scowls in the way that she does,
when I tell her about Celine.
She actually said that?

Yep, I say and reach
for another handful of popcorn
from the bowl between us
next to the family-size bag of M&M's.

We are family,
after all,
Mia and me.

Chosen family,
from that day when
both of us were first to put our toes
to the red line taped to the floor
in front of Miss Regina.

We go to different schools now
since ninth grade:
Mia's a private, all-girls school
two towns away.

Mine the public high school
near the center of our small town.

*Well, you know she's just jealous
because hers are so small.*
Mia smiles down
at her own pajama top,
the one with hedgehogs on it,
and adds,
Not that I should talk.

Oh please, I say.
I'd give anything to be your size.

Mia grows a wicked grin,
Don't you just wish,
you could give some to me?
I mean you don't want it,
and I could use it.

We are laughing and spilling M&M's
on the carpet in her room.
And I am thinking how awesome
it would be
if it were as easy as
plucking out wadded tissues
from one bra
and stuffing them into another.
No surgery required.

Last year, Mia actually did that
for her homecoming dance.

Only she was so self-conscious about
being lumpy   and discovered
that she abandoned the mission
halfway through
and flushed
her added padding
down the Girls' toilet.

We go back to watching *Moana*.
Even though we're old for it,
there is still everything to love
about Disney heroines,
their fierceness,
their independence,
their stories,
and their music.

20

We are closer to college
　　　　than to kindergarten,
but there are some things—
　　　　M&M's
　　　　　　　　movies
　　　　　　　　　　laughing over things that sting—
　　　　　　　　　　you never outgrow.

SOMETHING ELSE ABOUT THE DISNEY HEROINES

I like that
they are more than princesses.

I love that they are smart   confident   strong-willed
        that they speak their minds
                    and speak up for others
        that they solve problems others can't
                    and do things others are afraid to do.

But there is something
I don't love
about the Disney heroines.

I mean, I know they're cartoons.

But still.

They always have:
        Perfect hair
        Perfect skin
        Perfect tiny waists
        Perfectly proportioned breasts

I mean, Pocahontas with her fringe,
Elsa under her ice-blue gown,
Jasmine under her shimmery tulle,
Even Ariel in her seashells.

Not one bursting at the seams.

I can't help but notice
their breasts aren't much bigger
than their eyes.

FIRST FOOTBALL GAME

Under the stadium lights
everyone's breath
puffs   out like   ghosts
when they laugh.

Another week of school
has flown by, and
Mia and I are still
        floating
                about
                        Elite.

We leave our seats
to go grab hot cocoas
from the snack bar
because neither of us wore gloves
and our hands are freezing
even though it's only September.

I am always glad
for cold weather.

Cold weather means
        bulky sweatshirts,
                loose sweaters,
                        and layers
                                on layers.

Tonight, I added one of
Dad's fleece-lined
flannels on top of my hoodie.

Ahead of us in line
is a sturdy back
hunched forward
on crutches.

The back turns awkwardly.
Hey, Esme.
Todd McPherson,
who was in Biology
with me last year,
balances as he shuffles,
adjusts his crutches,
balances again.

A hulking black brace
is strapped around his knee
over his jeans.

What did you do?

Oh, I had knee surgery
this summer.
I was supposed to be off these
by now, he extends one crutch,
but the doctor says I need a couple more weeks.

That stinks.

Yeah, otherwise I'd be out there.
His head tips toward the field.

You play football? Mia asks.

Todd shakes his head
and a blush like fall leaves
creeps into his cheeks.

Oh, no, marching band.
I play the trumpet.
He diddles one set of fingers in the air

                          Air trumpet.

So, Esme, I think I'm going to be
in your AP U.S. History class.

Really?

Guidance took forever.
But I'll be there Monday.

Great, I say.
That'd be great.

Then the woman at the snack bar
calls, *Next,*
and Todd is turning away.
Before we step up to the counter,
Todd stuffs his Snickers bar
in his coat pocket,
turns back and says,
Well, see you Monday, Esme.

Mia nudges me in the ribs
with her pointy elbow.
And grins.

Her grin matches how I feel inside.

FROM THE STANDS

We drink our cocoa and
talk about the boys on the football team.
Mia still has a crush on
Devon Millhouse, even though I'm pretty sure
he's dating Angie LaValley.

Find out for me
if they're together,
Mia says.

It's hard meeting boys
when you go to an all-girl school.

For as long as we've been friends
Mia's wanted a boyfriend.
Not that she'll have the time
now that we're Elite.

We move on to talk about
the cheerleaders.
Two of them
are also Elite.

I point out Celine
who is one of the captains this year,
her not-more-than-a-handfuls
tucked away under her cropped uniform top.

I hate to admit it
but Celine is good.
Her kicks are as high
as the Elite girls.
She's strong and has good rhythm.

I can tell Mia
is trying to find
something to say about her.

Finally Mia says,
Wow, she sure does smile a lot.

Yeah, I say.

THE HEAT IS ON

in the car
when Mom
picks me up.

How was the game?

Good.

Under the streetlights
coming in the windows
the shadows under Mom's eyes
      are deep and dark
              like bruises.

So, she says,
hands tightening on the wheel,
her eyes on the road,
Grammy Jean is going to come stay with us
for a while.

Really?

The last time Grammy Jean came
the visit was cut short.

Yes, so she can help out.
Dad's going to need surgery
to straighten out his back.

Surgery?

I don't mean to,
but I think about Todd,

his knee in that brace that
looked like a torture device.

Will the surgery work?

Mom says, *I sure hope so.*

SURGERY

I spend a lot of time
thinking about surgery.

Specifically
reduction mammoplasty.

Aka
breast reduction surgery.

It's a secret thought
I haven't shared with anyone
not even Mia.

And now
with Dad needing surgery
I know it will have to stay
secret
a little while longer.

SATURDAY AT THE STUDIO

It's our last Saturday
on our own
before classes begin
next week.

Next week
we'll be Elite.
But for now we
are just Mia and Esme,
two best friends
who love to dance.

```
                        d
                          a
        DA               n
        NCE   c
d a n c e LOVe2
        DAN
    d a n CE
    a           2 l
        n           o
        c           v
            E
```

```
                    DA
                    NCE
            love2dance2love
                    DAN
                d a n CE
            love2        2love
```

MIA ON POINTE

Mia loves ballet.
    And she's perfect for
    pointe.

Small and sinewy
    tiny waist
        small chest
            powerful long legs
                knees that curve backward
                    large feet.

Like two points on a compass
    she dances circles around the map of the studio
        bend
            and dip
                and arc.

I gave up ballet
        around the same time
        I let go of tap.

By sixth grade
the Lycra of my leotard
strained across my chest.
Every part of me
    had grown thicker,
my waist
    my thighs
                my ankles, even.

And my boobs.

But Mia stayed small
            stayed soft
                        stayed tender
                                    Perfect for pointe.

Now I focus on lyrical
still beautiful
still powerful
allowing me motion
                    and emotion
just not leaving me
            teetering
            TOP HEAVY
                    on
                    toe
                    tips.

OUR OWN HEROINE

We both love
Misty Copeland,
principal dancer with the American Ballet Theatre.

She is the both of us.

Top heavy like me.
     Biracial like Mia.

Grew up without money like me
     Dances en pointe like Mia.

We both love
     her power
     her strength
     her determination.

Through Misty
we are reminded of
everything we can be

if we just work hard enough.

DINNER AT MIA'S

After our time in the studio
I text Dad
to check on him,
and to ask if I can eat over at Mia's.

Mom will be home
from the restaurant in half an hour,
probably with tacos
again.

She gets one free meal
and I know she doesn't eat
during her shift so that
she can bring it
home for us.
The cook, Antonio,
knows about Dad's accident
and always gives Mom extra.

Dad answers,
Have fun.

Mia's mom slips off her suede boots
on the mat near their door.
*What do you girls feel like
for dinner?*

I have a feeling
I could name any food
in the world
and Mia's mom
would get it on my plate.

Mia's parents
always drink wine
with dinner.
And they get
takeout
A LOT.
Her mom asks,
How about Mexican?

Maybe Mia
sees me flinch
or maybe the groan
in my head
was audible just to her,
because Mia answers,
How about pasta?
From Alfredo's?

That sounds amazing,
I chime in.

Pasta it is,
Mia's mom says.

I get chicken alfredo,
so creamy, so rich
I save half
for Dad to have
the next day.

MONDAY

Todd McPherson has
light brown eyes,
so light they are almost green.

As promised,
here he is Monday morning
in AP U.S. History, APUSH,
on his crutches
tilting his head
at the desk next to mine.

Is anyone sitting here?

Somebody (Jordan Gillespi, maybe?)
was sitting there last week,
but she's not here now.

I don't think so.

He maneuvers around the seat
lowers his tall frame,
awkward, stiff
because of the brace on his leg.
He leans his crutches against his desk.

Mr. Nash puts a syllabus in front of Todd.
You haven't missed much, he says.

Todd tells him thanks,
and pretends to look over
the syllabus.

But I catch him
stealing a glance at me.

I smile.
And he smiles back.

MIND CHOREOGRAPHY

Sometimes when I hear
a new song
on the radio,
I imagine choreography.

Moves I'd make
    here
        and
            here
                and there.

I see the movements in my mind,
feel the music
like a vibration rippling through me.

Like now, in Mia's car,
her mom driving
us to the studio.

My mom is working,
another extra shift
at the restaurant.

Dad was in the dog chair
when I left.
He promised not to get up
until someone got home.

Last week
Mom came home
to find Dad
lying on his side
on the floor
after he tried to get up
but couldn't.

The song ends,
my mind choreography fades.
We are here,
for our first night
with the Elite team.

FIRST CLASS

Twelve girls total.
No more, no less.

Mostly seniors.
An occasional junior.
But never, before now,
a sophomore.
Let alone two.

We are rare birds,
Mia and me.

When we cross over the threshold,
we bring with us
an unintended chill
that settles over the studio.

The other girls pause,
a break in their stretching
to look and
then look away.

The chatter that bubbled
warm in the room
dies.

The girls stretch
in silence.

Mia and I go to a corner,
put our bags down
and get busy stretching.

Across from me, Erin presses
her legs out on either side of her,
torso down to the floor.

Our glances meet in a flicker.
She shoots an icy glare at me.

I take stock of the dancers in the room.
I know these girls, the way they know me,
from recitals, performances, competitions.
I've danced with them.
They've danced with me.

Now an invisible line
has been taped across the floor
separating

us

from

them.

Kendall's voice
breaks the stillness.
I think if I was Jane, I'd quit, too.

Reagan adds,
It's her senior year.
What a slap in the face.

Alyssa says, *And poor Taryn,*
back down to Juniors.

I am on my feet,
trying to focus on my side bends.
Mia is still on the floor.
But we get the message.
Of course.
We have displaced
two of their own.

Brooke steps toward our spot.

Her eyes glance down at Mia
and then at me.

How good could you be?
she says
loud enough for everyone to hear.

Then Miss Regina enters,
clapping.

We are,
all of us,
lining up.

We will warm up.
And somehow,
we will dance together
as a team.

LANDING WRONG

How was it?
Mom asks when she picks me up.
She is wearing her uniform
and the car smells like fajitas.

Mia is already in her mom's car.

Okay.

Just okay?
She peers at me.
I turn away.

Dance
has always been
where I belonged.
Even when
my chest grew
(and grew)
my legs
carried the weight.

Tonight's class was okay.
We didn't stumble,
or trip.
Mia and I,
we held our own
carried our weight.

But nobody talked to us.
Acknowledged us.

The senior girls are getting into their cars.
I don't say anything.

Mom adds,
Well, it was just the first class.

She means well.
But when I think of
nine more months of classes like this,
three times a week,
the words land wrong.

Like a twisted ankle
my heart turns over.

Those words,
just the first class,
make me wince.

QUESTIONS LIKE HORNWORMS

This summer, the tomatoes
in Mom's garden were demolished.
Hornworms.
They start off small and grow.
So green and camouflaged,
at first you don't notice them.
You notice the destruction.
The ravaged tomatoes.

Brooke's question,
hours later,
has eaten into my brain.

HOW GOOD COULD YOU BE?

It gnaws at me,
a terrifying green worm
breaks the tender skin
begins to bore into me
Until I am questioning:

How good am I?

RARE
(OR NOT-SO-RARE) BIRDS

Mia,
fine-boned
small-framed,
a hummingbird that
dips and darts
from bloom to bloom,
an iridescent swipe of green in the sky.

Esme,
solid
thick-breasted,
meaty,
a blue jay that dives from
branch to branch,
a flash of blue against a leafy canopy.

The two of us,
we are not always well-matched
on the dance floor.
Not as a mirrored pair.

But sometimes
it works.
Me, the blue jay,
a power dancer
matched
with the grace, the lightness of
Mia, the hummingbird.

In friendship, too,
we are not a mirrored pair.

Mia goes to a school
where a uniform is required—
she can only wear her
lululemon leggings
on weekends.

I go to public high school,
and the only thing I've ever
purchased from lululemon
is a headband.

Both only children
who found a sister
in dance class
when we were four.

Even then, Mia's tap shoes
were shiny with a crisp ribbon.
Mine were from the donation bin,
dull and scuffed,
frayed ends on the ribbon.
But with some shoe polish and a new ribbon,
Mom made those shoes shine like Mia's.

And never once
did the shoes being
shiny new or
gently used
matter.

We are birds of a feather
as different
as a hummingbird
and a blue jay.

Not symmetrical,
but maybe complimentary,
on the dance floor and
in friendship.

ODE TO THE MUSTARD SANDWICH

Mom hasn't been to
the grocery store in a while.

The shelves in the fridge
look like a party no one came to.

A bottle of ketchup,
soy sauce,
Italian dressing,
mustard.
A few slices of bread.

On the counter,
there is a bag of pinto beans
and a can of store brand
diced tomatoes
that Mom will cook
with the last of the garden kale
for dinner tonight.

Last week, when she cooked this meal,
she said, *Pinto beans
have a lot of protein.*

That is dinner,
but I need to pack
lunch for school.

I grab two slices of bread,
and the mustard.

Mustard has more substance,
more heartiness
than ketchup.

Bright
and
zippy.
I decide right then,
it's my favorite condiment.

I know most people
love ketchup.
But mustard,
its unsung cousin,
wins the crown.

It adds texture
and tang.
Ketchup only adds
sweetness.

I just hope no one notices
that all I've brought
for lunch is
a mustard sandwich.

ZOE McKIM

I see Todd McPherson
with Zoe McKim.

They are talking
on their way to class
        her straight red hair
        flames out behind her.

She is beautiful
with her green eyes
and fine freckles sprinkled
like glitter over her nose.

She wears black jeans
ripped in all the right places
and on her T-shirt, some rock band
I don't recognize.

They get on the elevator.
Zoe holds the door
while Todd maneuvers inside
on his crutches.

Kids using crutches get a special key
to the elevator.
You can choose one person to ride with you
in case you need help carrying stuff.

Todd chose Zoe as his person.

The two of them
always seem to be together.
How did I not notice before?

My heart sinks
as I climb the stairs.

I SIT WITH ANGIE

at lunch.
We know each other
from dancing Juniors together
last year.

We miss you at Juniors, Angie says.
I smile and say,
I miss you guys, too.
And realize for the first time
how true that is.

How's it going on Elite?
And there's an echo
in my head,
HOW GOOD COULD YOU BE?

Good, I lie. I add,
You know, it's hard,
But good.

She nods, like this is the answer
she expected.

What kind of sandwich is that?
Angie asks.

Oh, it's mustard
and turkey,
I lie (again).
Thin sliced.

She looks like
she might say something else, so
I ask her how things are going
with Devon.
I owe Mia an update, after all.

It works.
Angie is off:
He is soooo sweet. I
wish he was in this lunch period. We
only have two classes together . . .
I guess they're
still dating.
Mia will be disappointed.

I finish off my sandwich
while she talks.
The mustard is good
but maybe not as hearty
as I hoped.

Angie holds up an apple.
Red and shiny.
McIntosh.
You want my apple?
I'm not going to eat it.

Sure, I say
casually.

I take a bite
that crunches too loud.
I taste fall
and a hint of shame.

CONVERSATION I OVERHEAR #2

That night
Mom's voice
sounds small.
Like it's being drowned out
in a storm.

Maybe I should apply
for assistance?

Assistance?
The edge in Dad's voice scrapes against
the walls of our house.

Yes, like
food stamps.

We don't need
to do that.
Once my workers' comp
clears . . .

But we don't know when
that will happen.
My paycheck is not enough.

We don't need
to do that.
It'll clear soon.

I hear Mom's footsteps
heading down the hallway.
Hear her say,
more to herself
than to Dad,
Well, we need to eat now.

And something about
how she says it—
with an edge of her own—
tells me
Mom is applying
for assistance
anyway.

NEXT MORNING

Mom's made oatmeal
on the stove.
The kitchen smells
like the first morning
the heat is on
and
cinnamon.

I'm calling the school today,
Mom says as she puts
a steaming bowl
in front of me,
to sign you up for the
free lunch program.

There are sliced bananas,
mixed in, cooked
until the bananas are
warm
and
soft.

I cradle the bowl
in both hands for a moment,
inhaling all that it has to offer.

And when I spoon
it in my mouth,
the oatmeal
tastes as good
as the kitchen
smells.

DRESSING ROOM MIRRORS

A dressing room mirror
is a fun house mirror,
only it's not fun.

Mia's voice travels
through the wall
between us.

Oh, this one is so cute!
You have to see it.

Okay, I say,
one sec.

I step
       and
              squeeze
and
      hoist
           and
                  shimmy
and
      tug
           and
                lift
and
still

in the fluorescent lights
I stand
bulbous
       and
            glowing white

                 like some translucent
                          sea creature belonging to the deep.

COME SEE

Mia's voice calls.

I peek out,
clutching my T-shirt
to my chest
covering
all
that
cleavage.

There is Mia.
Looking at herself
in the aisle mirror.

Even under the harsh lights
her warm skin
glows
her small, muscled form,
turning from side to side
to catch a glimpse
of herself
from every
angle.

The pink bikini fits
her perfectly.
Just like every
dance costume
at every fitting
every year.
Like every pair of cute pajamas,
every sweater,
every tank top,
every
thing.
Perfectly.

And then
her afterthought,
How about yours?

I shake my head,
The top is too small,
I say,
my voice getting small, too.

I lower the T-shirt

                   for

                        a

                                second.

      Already my nipples
      are about to play
            peek-a-boo
      and spring out of the thin fabric.

*Maybe you could
get a bigger size top?*

I don't answer because
really, I know
      there's no way I will buy
      this swimsuit
      which I would never wear
      with money I do not have.

The only way
a bikini enters
my realm of possibility
would be
after a reduction surgery.
Who buys a swimsuit in
October anyway?

Only the girls who look good
from every angle
(even in a fun house mirror)
and who have trips
to Bermuda planned
for December.

And that is not me.

WHAT LOVE SMELLS LIKE

Mia and I sip
Starbucks (her treat) and
walk through the mall,
store by store
until her hands
are loaded
with shopping bags
in every color.

In PINK
Mia picks out
pairs of cute undies
and we move on to
lotions and fragrances.

I spray the tester for the perfume *Love*,
which I've always liked.

On my wrist, the scent is
sweet and delicate.

It reminds me of
walking through a field
of wildflowers, the sun
on my face,
not a care in the world.

I love this scent
I confide in Mia.

*You should totally
get it.*

But even the smallest bottle
is way out of my price range.

I think she realizes this
and changes the subject.
Why do you think they call it Love?

I shrug.
Perfume companies
are always trying to come up with
one-word names, something
powerful   or   emotional   or romantic.

We wait in line
so Mia can pay.
And I keep smelling my wrist
thinking this could be
exactly
what love smells like.

WE HEAD TO THE EXIT

Mia's dad will be here soon
to pick us up.

The mall is warm
       and I take off my sweatshirt
       to tie it around my waist
       even though I only have
       a thin, cropped T-shirt underneath.

As we walk,
I catch an older woman
looking at me
and shaking her head.
Disapproving.
I can tell she doesn't like how
I'm dressed,
that I should cover up my body
maybe hide my big boobs.

I try to ignore her.

I nod at Mia's shopping bags.
Want me to carry some of those?

Oh, sure. That'd be great.

Mia hands me a few.

And I think,
she doesn't know
what it's like
to not be able
to buy something.

To not have the newest iPhone,
or seven different pairs of Nikes
on a shelf in your closet.

She doesn't know
what it's like
to wear no-name
shirts and leggings

To buy your bras and underwear
in bulk from Walmart.

And then
I think she knows
what I'm thinking,
must see it on
my face,
like an unflattering
shade of eye shadow.

I think she knows
I'm judging her.
I don't mean to,
but I do.

Maybe I overdid it?
she asks with a small laugh.

But before I can answer
we hear
a low whistle
and a husky voice say

Whoa.

A group of three guys
has stopped
to stare at us
              at me
                    at my chest.

We keep walking.
Avoid eye contact.

Mia rolls her eyes.
Ugh, she mutters.
Sorry, Esme.

Silently
I hand back her bags
so I can untie my sweatshirt
and put it back on.

JOB HUNTING

I understand
why they call it job hunting.

Like casting a fishing line
or throwing a spear,
I am filling out job applications
at every place
within walking distance
of school.

I could pour coffee
        at Dunkin'
or make sandwiches
        at Subway
or scoop ice cream
        at Spindler's Candy Shop
        next to the library.

I haven't told my parents.
I know Dad would say
        school is my job
And Mom would look
        sadder than I could handle right now.

It doesn't matter, anyway.

No fish is biting at my hook,
no antelope running toward my spear.

I fill out each application
neatly and
double-check my
phone number,
but still
no one calls.

66

NEXT CLASS

If we could go to class
and just dance,
be a part of Elite,
finally,
everything would be fine.

But we enter
a cold room,
where ten pairs of
cold eyes
follow us.

Brooke doesn't waste time,
steps toward us,
her footfalls pounding.
A few girls follow.
If you respected this team,
you'd give up
your spots
and go back down
to Juniors where you belong.

Mia looks green,
and I feel my face
grow hot.

I want to speak,
to say out loud,
so the whole room hears,
That's not happening.

But I don't.
I turn away,
drop my bag against the back wall
and start to stretch.

Mia follows.

We don't say a word.

Don't worry,
Brooke taunts,
give it another week
and you'll be wishing
you were back
where you belong.

I guess proving
ourselves to Miss Regina
was the easy
part.

AFTER CLASS

Mia and I sit
in the backseat
while her mom
drives us home.

We are quiet,
as Mia pulls out
her phone.

Mine buzzes
with a text:

*Maybe we should
go back to Juniors.*

I don't look up,
don't want to see
the defeat
in my best friend's
eyes.

I focus on my reply:

No way.

GRAMMY JEAN

Grammy Jean's earrings
are as big as
her personality.

(She says she's
held onto them
since the eighties and
never plans to
give them up.)

Right now
in her hug
her arms around me
the gold wire shapes
hanging from her ears
tangle in my hair.

When we pull apart
I extract myself
carefully from
the geometric prison.

Sometimes the earrings are
disks of gold or silver or
plastic in brightly colored shapes or
even feathers.

Once, she told me
how the big earrings remind her
of 1989,
the year
everything changed.

1989

The year Grampa Tom
died.

Way before I was born,
when Dad was only
fifteen, like I am now.

Your dad, Grammy Jean likes to say, *is a lot
like Grampa Tom.*
Looks like him.
Talks like him.
Thinks like him.

After she lost Grampa Tom
she kept going
because she had my dad—
her only child.
And because she found
something to give her strength.
Aerobics.
Aerobics was super popular in the eighties.
Like Zumba, Grammy Jean always says.
She found strength
through movement,
motion,
in dance beats.

I've seen the old photos of her
in a body-hugging leotard,

curving around her full chest
(not quite as full as mine).
And leg warmers
with white Reeboks,
like the ones Mia bought for school
this year.

Grammy Jean used to dance
before she got married
and became a housewife.
Somehow, she told me,
working her body
again in aerobics class
reminded her of who she was
and that she was strong.
     Aerobics saved me
     is how Grammy Jean puts it.

And I think I get it—how moving your body,
pushing it beyond what
your mind thinks possible,
feeling the thunder of music
rumble through you—
there's a strange kind of power.
But I wonder
how that sort of thing
can save you.

BEAUTY IS IN THE EYE OF THE GRANDMOTHER

Oh Esme!
Grammy Jean says,
Let me get a good look
at you.

She holds me by both hands
and leans back to look at me
like I am a work of art.

Beautiful, so beautiful.

I am in jeans and an old T-shirt
and I have a zit on my chin
that no amount of cover-up
can hide.

But my grandmother
thinks I am
the *Venus de Milo*
(only with arms
and bigger boobs).

A PRETTY PENNY

You have a gorgeous figure, Esme,
Grammy Jean says,
voluptuous
        and
                athletic.

Why do people
(even people that I love)
feel like they have
the right
to comment on my body?

And what does that even
mean?

That I am equal parts

        Playboy Bunny

                  and

                        Serena Williams?

Grammy adds,
like I should
be grateful,
Women would pay
a pretty penny
to look like you.

She doesn't know
that I dream
     of the reverse—
     that I would pay a pretty penny
     to shrink down this top half of me.
I know she means
this as a compliment.

But it doesn't feel
that way
to me.

OUT OF SYNC

In dance class
the questions on my mind
trip me up.

Instead of fluid,
I am faltering on my feet,
forgetting for a half a second
what comes next.

A small stutter
a single hesitation
sets my mind spinning.

It's not just the weight of my chest.
It's the weight of worry that
presses down on my heart,
that tricks my brain
trips my feet.

I see Miss Regina's lips
set in a stern line.

HOW GOOD COULD YOU BE?
plays in my head,
ties a knot around my heart.

When you dance,
you move not just with your body.
But with your mind
with your heart.

If any one is out of alignment
        body
                heart
                        mind
no matter the rhythm
no matter the beat
the dancer falls out of sync.

And a dancer out of sync

sinks.

FOR A LITTLE FUN

Grammy Jean has made
black bean soup for dinner
with cornbread.
She's already
given
Dad his.

Dad watches TV in his chair
while the three of us eat
at the kitchen table.

Mom still wears her
restaurant uniform,
smelling like smoky cilantro and jalapeños.

Hey, Grammy Jean says,
I know what we should do.
Let's all get manicures
this weekend.

I say,
without thinking,
Fun! I haven't had
a manicure in so long.

Mom looks up from her bowl,
and her face turns murky
dark like the soup.

It's true.
I haven't been in years,
since Mia's birthday party in seventh grade.
She and her mom go every other week,
for some kind of miracle gel that
hardens into a slick shell on their nails.

78

I know Mom will say no,
that we can't afford it.
And she is right.

I insist, Grammy Jean says
to Mom.
You deserve to do something for yourself.
My treat.
Mom looks at me.
I keep my face neutral.
But I think she sees that I'd like to go.

And she says,
That could be fun.

She says it with a sad smile,
like she'll probably regret it.

Grammy Jean's
big pink earrings shimmy
with excitement.
She says,
with a wink,
to me,
What are credit cards for,
if not for a little fun.

PROM 1993

Mom has a simple black dress
she wears for funerals.
And a flowered one
for weddings.

But on her dresser, there's an old photo
of Mom and Dad
from high school,
their faces washed clean
of twenty-something years of worry.

Printed at the top of the photo:

Prom 1993
Hold onto the Night

Dad in a rented tux,
and Mom in emerald green,
a sequined gown
that drapes to the floor
and hugs her curves,
her perfectly ordinary chest
balanced evenly with her hips.
Her long dark hair
swept up.

Their smiles as bright
as the huge chandelier that twinkles
behind them,
showering sparks of light
that get caught
in the sequins on Mom's dress and
in the glimmer of my parents' eyes.

80

When I was little, I thought
Mom looked like a movie star.

Once when I was in middle school
I asked if she still had that dress.
She laughed,
God no.
Why would I need a dress
like that?
Most days
she wears her uniform:
a black button-down shirt
Sombrero's embroidered in red thread
on the breast pocket,
black shoes
tan pants
green apron,
     as in forest green,
      dull and stained in places,
not like those emerald sparkles.

At night
she sleeps in Dad's old T-shirts
and in the garden
she wears jeans or cargo shorts
depending on the season.

Sequins and chandeliers belong to the past.
But I wish there was
some way for her to
HOLD ONTO THE NIGHT
the magic of it
from 1993.

THE ELITE TWELVE (AND OUR NICKNAMES FOR THEM)

1. Brooke (Senior): Queen Bitchiness Herself (evil genius of mean looks and insulting comments)
2. Liv (Senior): The Quiet One (too quiet to tell what she is thinking)
3. Erin (Senior): Dimples (blond cheerleader who is the top of the pyramid)
4. Kendall (Senior): Rebel K (hair dyed black and a nose ring that Miss Regina makes her remove for competitions)
5. Catie (Senior): The Triple Threat (dances, sings, and acts—gets the lead in my school's theater productions every year)
6. Reagan (Senior): The Flyer (cheerleader #2, can do acrobatics)
7. Abbey (Senior): Triple A, aka Amazing Airy Abbey (super high leaps)
8. Alyssa (Senior): Bangs (because she has bangs, goes to Mia's school)
9. Sofia (Junior): Soul Star (elegant, soulful dancer, also goes to Mia's school)
10. Faith (Junior): The Nice One (nice to everyone, so nice even Brooke leaves her alone)
11. Mia (Sophomore): SBP (Small But Powerful, bad knee but good heart)
12. Esme (Sophomore): Serena Bunny (Serena Williams meets Playboy Bunny, plagued with big boobs and self-doubt)

MISS REGINA

reminds us of our
competition schedule.

Three major events.
One in February
One in March
One in April

It goes without saying
(Miss Regina says anyway)
that those of you
new to the team
should NOT expect
to get a solo
or even a duet or trio.

Miss Regina adds
That said,
we dance as a team—
each of us only as good
as the girl next to her.

which just gives Brooke
another excuse to shoot
daggers at me and Mia.

83

SUBTLE

Brooke's shoulder
into my back
a jab so subtle,
no one else notices
as we line up.

It makes my heart
kick in my chest.

I make eye contact.

She glares.

I look away.

NOT-SO-SUBTLE

Later in class
Brooke finds a moment
between songs

to sidle up next to me
and whisper
in my ear:

*Let's just hope
you don't get
two black eyes.*

At first
I think she's
threatening me.

But then she
smirks and looks
at my chest

and that's when
I realize it's
an insult.

WHEN WE GET OUR NAILS DONE

When we get our nails done,
I pick a purple shade,
but my cuticles bleed red.

When we get our nails done,
Grammy Jean chatters to anyone who listens,
but Mom says almost nothing.

When we get our nails done,
my fingertips shine in the lights overhead,
but I worry if they're dry.

When we get our nails done,
Grammy Jean's credit card is declined,
but she jokes that she always carries a spare.

When we get our nails done,
the second card goes through,
but Mom's silence is as sharp as the acetone smell in the salon.

When we get our nails done,
my fingertips shine and I feel like I'm worth it
but in the car, I notice my thumbnail is already smudged.

ON HOLD

Dad's surgery
waits on hold
like a forgotten phone call.

I've overheard enough
to know that it has to do with
the cost.

Something about
his workers' compensation
not being approved.

Mom is doing dishes
and Grammy Jean folds laundry.

Grammy Jean says,
*Let's tell them
we're getting a lawyer.*

Mom shakes her head.
*How would we ever
afford that?*

*You don't actually hire one.
It's just what you say.*

It's not fair
that money decides everything,
whether a man can
get well
walk
work
again.

I speak up.
*What about
pro bono, you know,
lawyers who work for free.
I saw it on TV.*

That's an idea,
Grammy Jean says.

*Nothing
in this world
is free,*
Mom says,
signaling that
this conversation
is over.

MONEY IS A WALL

Sometimes I like to think
of all the things
I'd do
if money were no object.

If I had all the money
in the world, I would:

Buy five new pairs of jazz shoes
Go on a shopping spree for dance shorts
Buy that perfume from the mall
But then I think about Mia and Mia's family.
Wait . . . aim bigger.

I would:
Take a trip to Bermuda
Buy my parents a big, beautiful house
with a pool!
And a brand-new car
to replace our junky one!
And while I'm at it, I'll buy a new car for me!

And of course, I'd:
Pay for college
Pay for dad's surgery
Pay for my surgery—if I do it.

Money is a wall

on one side
those who have it
        on the other
        those who don't.

Sometimes those who don't
break free
climb the wall
to the other side.

And I suppose
Sometimes the opposite happens.
Those who have it
fall from their side.

But it seems to me
Climbing
is harder
than Falling.

LITTLE KID LESSONS

At least Wednesday nights
are still fun.
The little kids remind me
why I fell in love with
dance in the first place.

They leap and hop
and twirl like
baby bunnies
or kittens.
All joy.

Sometimes they rush
to be around Zara,
who knows the positions
by heart, and the one
Miss Regina praises most.
Very nice, Zara.

They push
to stand next to Zara
as if by being close to her,
they will shine brighter.

Little Aubrey is the clueless one.
The one who can't keep up
who stares into space,
who sometimes
chews her hair
while they sit
crisscross applesauce.

But when Aubrey's mom
brings cupcakes for her birthday,
the girls crowd and push
to stand next to Aubrey.

Their alliances shift,
just like that.

And it gives me an idea.

WE FORM A PLAN

After the little girls
skip out of the room,
and Aubrey's mom
has handed out the cupcakes,
including one for me
and one for Mia,
I grab Mia's arm.

*We need to be
strategic about this,*
I say as we bite
into our cupcakes.

What do you mean?
Mia asks,
licking frosting from her thumb.

*Just because
Brooke is the loudest—*

—and bitchiest, Mia adds

Right—
*Doesn't mean
she speaks for the whole team.*

I hope that this
is true, at least.

We need to shift alliances.

I hold up my half-eaten cupcake.

93

I don't get it.
We bring them cupcakes?
Mia asks.

No, we tip the scales.
We don't need everyone to like us,
just one or two.

We finish our cupcakes.
Then we form a plan.

ONLY IT'S NOT MUCH OF A PLAN

The goal is not to let Queen Bitchiness run the show.

To do that:

1. We need allies.
2. Triple Threat Catie and Soul Star Sofia are our best bets.
3. My assignment is to find a way to connect with Triple Threat.
4. Since Soul Star goes to Mia's school, Mia's assignment is to connect with her.
5. Get them on our side first.
6. With their help, get more girls on our side.
7. Then everyone will see the Queen for who she really is.

CENTER OF THE UNIVERSE

At the next class,
Miss Regina announces
that Brooke will solo
in the lyrical group number.
When we run the number
the Queen emerges center stage
and dances
while we move to the outer edges.

It is the worst possible
metaphor,
like she is the sun
and we all
revolve around her.

She is firmly
at the center of the universe
and, allies or not,
we are planets
spinning mercilessly
at the outer edge.

GROUNDED

By design,
the bones of birds are hollow.
Weightless, feathered
the air lifts them skyward.

Tonight,
I cannot lift off
cannot propel
cannot catch the air
to reach the height I need.

The density of my bones,
the heavy flesh of me,
of my chest,
keeps me grounded.

Brooke's vulture eyes follow me everywhere.
Miss Regina's mouth pinches into a frown.
Neither one says anything.

They don't have to.

I hear them anyway.

CELINE'S IDEA OF PERFECT

The next day at school
Celine hasn't done the pre-lab
we had for homework.

We stand at our lab station
and I let her copy mine
because we just need
to get this done.

While I read the instructions,
she grimaces, putting
on her goggles.

I follow the steps,
and she hands me things.
At least she can
follow directions.

You're pretty smart, huh?

I shrug and say
Not really.
I just did the reading,
hoping she'll take the hint.

I bet you
get A's all the time.

I shrug again and say,
My parents are intense
about getting into college.

This is only part true.
They want me to get into college,
but they aren't too intense.

98

I decide how hard I work.
So I work hard.
For me.

You should totally come,
Celine says.

When I look up,
she grins.
To the Halloween party?
At Megan Matthison's?
It's going to be great—
costumes—
OMG—
You know who you should be?
That country lady
you know—
Dolly Parton!

She says it like it's the most
original idea she's had all year.
(It probably is.)

That would be perfect for you!

Yeah, I say,
Perfect.

WHEN I GET TO APUSH

Todd is sitting
at his desk
without crutches!

His knee is free
of the black torture device
and his leg is folded
under the desk
like normal.

Hey, no crutches!
I say sliding into my seat.

Yep, I'm free!
No more elevator,
no more having someone
carry my lunch tray.

My mind blinks
to Zoe with the fiery hair. Maybe
now she won't be around so much.

What are you
most excited to do
now that you're free?

Funny you should ask.
I heard there was a Halloween party
at Megan Matthison's on Saturday.
Could be fun?

Before I can even
enjoy the possibility that
Todd might be asking me
to go with him,
my mind double blinks
back to last period,
my conversation with Celine.

Todd must see my face fall.
Not a fan of Halloween?

I shake my head.
No, it's not that.
I'm just . . .

And then Mr. Nash
is reminding us of the test
on Friday,
and I am hoping
I didn't just scare away
my chance for a date
with Todd McPherson,
who is finally free of his crutches
and maybe also of Zoe.

GRAMMY JEAN PEELS AN ORANGE

When I get home from school
Grammy Jean is in the kitchen
      peeling an orange.
Dad is asleep in the dog chair.

Her fingers mesmerize,
      working the orange in her hands
      like it is clay to be molded.
She peels away the skin
      making a neat pile on the table.

She sees me and
knows right away
something is
on my mind.

There is no hiding anything
from Grammy Jean—
my dad must not have
gotten away with
much in high school.

I tell her about the
Halloween party,
and Celine's earth-shattering
idea that I should go
as Dolly.

Why? Grammy Jean asks.
Because you're big-busted?
(Who says that? Big-busted?
      Only Grammy Jean.)

Yup . . .

Hmm.
Grammy Jean keeps peeling.
Using her manicured nails
to pluck away the pith.

Do you know, Grammy Jean says,
every time I peel an orange
I think of my friend, Diane.
She taught accounting
at the local community college.
She was allergic to
        oranges.

Which is just a good reminder,
that humans, as a species,
can be allergic to anything.

One day, Diane was teaching,
and a student in the front row
had an orange.

Can you believe Diane didn't say anything?

Grammy waves the orange in front of her,
naked now, without its peel.

She kept teaching
as the woman peeled the orange.
Diane's nose itched.
Her throat scratched.
Her eyes started to water.
And still she said nothing.

She kept going,
until finally she had to excuse herself
to get some air.

It makes me think about
what they taught me
in a CPR class years ago.
Sometimes people who are choking
will run from a room,
instead of asking for help.
They are too embarrassed,
too polite to interrupt dinner.

And that's a good reminder,
that humans as a species,
are embarrassed by all the wrong things.

Listen to me.
Why am I telling you all of this, Esme?
she asks, handing me half the orange.

I shake my head and
stuff a slice in my mouth,
hoping I don't choke.

Stop
being
so
damn
polite.

And for godssake,
never let embarrassment
stand in the way
of what might be
a matter of
life or death.

LET ME TELL YOU

And let me tell you
something else:
one could do worse
than Dolly Parton.

That woman
has made her mark
on this world.

Do you know she gives
free books to toddlers
and band uniforms to high school kids?

She writes all her own songs
and came up from nothing,
poorer than poor.

Let me tell you,
she's
smart
funny
sassy
generous
and kind.

Anyone with half a head
of sense
should be proud to be
compared to
Dolly.

YES, GRAMMY

Dolly is great.
But that's not the point . . .

And I'm not sure
we're talking about
life or death here.

Grammy grabs the orange peels
and throws them
into the trash.

Oh Esme, honey . . .
Aren't we?

ALL THE NEXT DAY

Grammy Jean's
pep talk
plays in my head.

In Health class
Mrs. Bent talks
about BODY POSITIVITY.

She says it a little too loudly,
and writes it on the board in
big   capital   letters.

Next to me, Angie
inspects her fingernails.

I sink down
in my seat while
Mrs. Bent explains how
BODY POSITIVITY is really
about self-acceptance,
feeling good about how
we look.

*Think about all the good things
your body can do,*
she tells the class.

There is snickering
behind us
from the back row
of junior boys.

How many of you play sports?
    Hands go up.
How many of you dance or do karate or yoga or ride a bike or swim?
    More hands go up,
    Angie's and mine, too.

Mrs. Bent talks more about
how amazing the human body is.

Every time she says BODY POSITIVITY
her voice goes up an octave
and she points to the words on the board.

I hear the boys behind me
whisper, catch the words
I wish I didn't hear:

Hey
I'm POSITIVE
that if we could combine
Esme's rack
with Angie's ass
we'd have the perfect woman.

Angie turns around
and glares at them.

I keep my eyes forward
staring at the letters on the board
and thinking about
what Grammy Jean
meant by life or death
    but mostly considering whether
    it's possible to die
    from embarrassment.

WHEN I GET HOME FROM SCHOOL

I'm still fuming
about Health class and
how even after
Grammy Jean's talk
I couldn't tell those guys
to shut up.

Dad, in the dog chair,
tells me Grammy Jean
is out running an errand.

I get him some water and a snack
and head to my room
to start homework.

On my bed,
I'm greeted by a
fluffy
blond
wig.

And an envelope.

I open it,
and, no kidding,
the card has a drawing of
Dolly Parton's dimpled face,
and the caption:

WWDD?
What Would
Dolly Do?

Inside is my grandmother's handwriting:

Whatever you do,
just make sure
to be proud
of yourself.
I am always
proud of you.

Love,
Grammy Jean

But how can I
even think about being
Dolly now?

Then
　　　　something clicks.

Because I think
when Grammy Jean
said life or death,
she didn't mean
actual life or death
breathing versus choking.

I think it's about
not letting embarrassment
or other people's opinions
　　　　decide
　　　　what you
　　　　will
　　　　or
　　　　won't
　　　　do.

110

WWDD?

The rest of the costume
comes together
quickly.

I have a denim skirt
and a red plaid shirt to match the red lipstick
I wear for dance competitions.

Grammy Jean
scores a rhinestone belt
at the thrift store.

And Mia,
even though she thinks
I'm crazy,
loans me the cowboy boots
she bought

on her family's vacation
to a dude ranch in Texas last year.

*Are you sure
you can't come?*
I ask her again.
I'm not sure
I'll be brave enough
to actually go to the party
without Mia.

I wish I could,
but we've had these tickets
for the ballet for months.
Esme, Mia asks with
that worried look
she wears a lot now,
Are you sure
you want to do this?
Aren't you worried
some of the Elite girls
will be there?
It's occurred to me.
Reagan and Erin
are cheerleaders, like Celine.
On the other hand . . .

I'm kind of hoping Triple Threat
will be there, I say.
This could be my chance
to talk to her.

Mia nods.
But what will you do if
they say something
bitchy?

I guess I'll just
ask myself,
What Would Dolly Do?

112

NOTE IN MY LOCKER

I heard you
might be coming
to the Halloween party.

I hope so.

I'll try to find you.

     —T.M.

REGRET

Saturday morning's dance class
is one of our worst.
Mia and I both
struggle to keep up.

As the other dancers file out
Miss Regina calls
Esme. Mia. Come here please.

I glance at Mia
and see my own fear
reflected in her eyes.

Brooke is last to leave
and before she crosses the threshold,
she turns and lets a slow smile
play on her lips.

Miss Regina folds her arms
and looks from
me to Mia
Mia to me.

What's going on with the two of you?

*I don't think I've ever
seen you
so sloppy
so hesitant.
Where are the two dancers
from this summer?
The ones who showed me
they deserved to be on Elite?*

114

I shake my head
to clear it, open my mouth
but nothing comes out.

Mia finds the words for both of us,
Sorry, Miss Regina.
I guess we're just
adjusting.

Miss Regina looks to me.

I nod.

Well, the time for adjusting
is over, girls.
If you can't keep up on Elite,
I'll have no choice but to move you
back down to Juniors.

WHEN WE STEP OUTSIDE

We are silent.
I guess we're in shock.

The sun seems too bright.
The sky too blue.
Mia's eyes shine with tears.
What are we going to do, Esme?

I don't know
I whisper.
HOW GOOD COULD YOU BE?
hums in my brain, background music
to a new question:
Where are the two dancers
from this summer?

We can do this, I say.
We just need
to work harder,
like we did in the summer

The rush of a car engine startles us
as a dark grey sedan rips into the road in front of us.

The side window
rolls down.
Brooke is behind the wheel.

Hello, girls.
Have a nice talk
with Miss Regina?
Awww.
Don't worry.
I'm sure it'll get better.

She adds with a grin,
It can't get much worse.

116

PARTY TIME

Grammy Jean pulls down
Blagden Street.
It's not hard to spot Megan's house
because of all the cars.
As we get closer
we hear music booming.
After this morning's dance class
I thought about bailing on the party.
But Grammy Jean insisted
it might feel good
to be someone else
for a little while.

That, and the note from TM
in my locker, was enough
to get me here.

Grammy Jean looks me over,
saying I look gorgeous.

But I feel
exposed.

Under my plaid shirt,
a tank top helps to hold me in.
But it's less than my usual
number of layers.
And tight.
The plaid red and blue stripes
curve around me
and cinch down
to my waist
where I've knotted the shirt
to show my belly button.

There is no hiding
my chest
in this costume
and I suppose that is
the point.
Grammy Jean blows me a kiss
before she drives away.

My cowgirl boots
click on the walkway
to the door.
Tonight, I tell myself,
I'm not Esme
(who would shrink her boobs
in a heartbeat if possible).

Tonight
I am Dolly.

EYES

I step into the house
and almost
step right back out.

I feel
every pair of eyes,
from Minnie Mouse
and Mickey
to Timmy Turner
and Trixie
to the random
devil
angel
alien
Hulk
Cleopatra
Red M&M
and
zombie ballerina,
sizing me up.

Regret nips at
the heels of my borrowed boots.

I'm about to text
Grammy to come back
and get me,

until
        my
                eyes
                        meet
                              Kenny's.

KENNY, AS IN ROGERS

who isn't really Kenny
but Todd,
      as in McPherson.

He smiles
through
a beard
of
painted-on
white
and
black
hashmarks
as he makes
his way over.

Then, he is right
in front of me,
my costume
giving him
(and everyone else)
permission
to look me over.

I got your note,
I breathe.

I'm glad you came.
You look incredible,
Esme.
Or should I say Dolly?

I nod.
Are you . . . Kenny Rogers?

Ma'am
and he tips his
cowboy hat at me.

And even though
the music pulses to
a fast beat
instead of the
meandering wallow
of a country song,
Kenny
and
Dolly
dance.

LOVE THAT RED

The music
shifts
to something
slow.

And I move closer
to Todd,
who moves closer to me.

His hands
on my denim hips
his eyes
on my red red lips.

*You look good
in lipstick.*

Thanks, I say,
It's Love That Red.

He looks confused.

My chest presses against his,
and I don't think I mind.
I keep talking
so I don't have to think.

That's what it's called,
    the color
        Love That Red.

*We wear it for
dance competitions.*

I feel Todd
breathing,
and he's tall,
and we're swaying.

*Hey, how did you
know I was going to be Dolly?*

*I heard something
from that girl Celine,
your lab partner.
She's in my study hall*

*So I took a chance.
Thought it would be fun
to surprise you as Kenny.*

He shrugs,
and my hands
lift with his sturdy
shoulders.

*Well, I guess
I should give you my number
so next time you can text me.
I would hate to
leave you hanging . . .*

I can't believe it—
I'm pretty sure I'm flirting!
Maybe being Dolly
has its advantages.

I'd like that,
Todd says

And my eyes
look into his
light brown
almost green
ones.

And I can tell by the way
Todd keeps
looking at my lips,
that he
Loves
That
Red
too.

THE PARTNER I DIDN'T CHOOSE

Todd and I
go into the kitchen
to get
something to drink.

There's beer
but we both grab Cokes.

Celine,
who appears much
more comfortable
wearing black cat ears
than Chemistry goggles,
sees me and shrieks.

She rushes over
screeching,

YOU

LOOK

A-MAZ-ING!

Kendall,
doesn't Esme
look   A-MAZ-ING?

And I see that she
means Kendall,
as in Nose Ring Kendall
as in Elite Rebel K.

Kendall, in a
Captain America T-shirt
that shows off a
belly button ring
(I wonder for a minute
if there's a third piercing
I don't know about),
nods at me,
a small smile
tugs at her lips
as she looks me over.

Dolly?

I nod.

Ballsy, Kendall says.

OMG—
Celine breaks in,
*And you are that
country guy!*
She waggles her fingers at Todd.

Kenny Rogers, Todd says.

Celine
grabs my hands,
and I have a feeling
she has been drinking
something besides
soda.

You know,
Celine announces
to the entire kitchen,
*I would be failing
Chemistry without Esme.*

That's not true,
I tell her
(even though it probably is).

She is a lifesaver,
Celine says
throwing an arm
around my shoulders.

And Kendall
smiles and says,
Nice.

Whether or not
she knows it,
Celine may have
just repaid
the favor.

TEXT WITH MIA

How was the ballet?

> *Sooo amazing. Just what I needed.*
> *How was the party?*

It ended up being really fun.
Todd came as Kenny Rogers
bc he knew I was Dolly.

> *Awwww!*

Erin and Reagan were there.
But it was fine.
No Catie, but Kendall.
Think I found a possible ally.

IN MIA'S BASEMENT

Mia agrees
when I say we can't just
find allies. We have to
WORK HARDER.

We've added Monday night
practices in her basement studio
to our plan.

To become the dancers
from this summer
we have to work as hard
as we did then.

Mia's basement is finished
with a dance studio on one end
and an entertainment room
on the other.

We run through the
contemporary number
and some of the lyrical.

Here, with only Mia,
I can ignore the
swinging of my chest
as I leap, focus on the other parts of me
the muscles in my quads
and calves,
my biceps stretching
as my arms lift.

Here I can be the dancer
I know I am.

Mia and I practice for two hours
until my shoulders burn
the way they did this summer
and she is limping on her wrapped knee.

SOMETIMES

Sometimes when I'm
not so focused
on technique
and my mind is wandering
away from me

I'm thinking about
Dad, waiting in the dog chair,
wondering if he'll be in pain forever.

I'm thinking about
Mom and the shadows under her eyes,
her sighs, heavy, weary, when she gets home from the restaurant.

about
money
and what it means if we don't have enough.

about
surgery
how much it costs, how much it must hurt

And then
I'll create my own mini
choreography to a really great song

high chaîné

    low chaîné

        into a

            b a r r e l e d calypso

       and tuck and roll

and all those thoughts
tumble away.

ADORABLY PINK

After school
I run into Todd
carrying a guitar case
in the hall.

You play guitar?

Guitar, Bass, Trumpet, Flügelhorn.

Flügelhorn? Is that even real?
Isn't that from Dr. Seuss?

He laughs,
and almost without missing a beat
recites:

The flügelhorn I love to play
I play it each and every day!
Why do I love it?
    I just can't say!
But I will play it anyway!

Did you just make that up? I ask

And Todd shrugs and says *Yeah* and
his ears turn adorably pink.
Hey, he says, *I'm heading to*
the band room.
To jam
with some friends
Sam Owen Christian Zoe
Want to come?

I'm about to say no

133

(I'm supposed to be at the library
researching my Shakespeare paper),
but then I realize
maybe I should go
if Zoe is going to be there.

JAMMING

Sam Owen Christian Zoe
are setting up
tuning their instruments.

Zoe is gorgeous as ever,
with her hair pulled into a messy bun.

They seem excited to see me,
even Zoe,
who flashes me a bright smile.

Todd tells me
they might have an actual gig
lined up.

Sam's uncle
knows a guy
and they might get to play
in some Battle of the Bands
at a community center in
the next town over.

Todd
       strums his guitar.

Sam
       hammers on drums.

Owen
       plinks at the keyboard.

Christian
       plucks the bass.

And Zoe
> belts on the microphone.

> Her voice is smooth and rich,
> reminding me of real hot chocolate,
> the kind you make on the stove
> with milk and cocoa powder.

They play
> everything under the sun
> hard rock, folk, blues, pop,
> and each song blazes hot.

Then I recognize
> a Jim Croce song.
> My dad listens to Jim Croce
> because his dad used to listen to it.

And I am swaying along in my seat
wishing it wouldn't be weird
for me to get up and dance.

RESEARCH

During a break
in their practice
Zoe comes over to me.

She pulls the scrunchy from her hair
and it falls like a curtain around her shoulders.

It's great to finally hang out with you, Esme.
You're all Todd wants to talk about lately.

A thrill runs through me.
I don't quite know
what to say.
But Zoe keeps smiling,
He was so happy
that you showed up at the Halloween party.

Yeah, that was fun, I say.
You didn't go?

My ex-girlfriend
was going to be there.
It was a whole
thing.

She shakes her head
and keeps talking.

Anyway, Todd's a great guy.
            We've known each other forever.
His mom is like best friends with my mom.
            He's kind of like another brother to me.

And I feel like I've stumbled into
a different kind of research—
not about Shakespeare.

but definitely
good to know.

A WARNING

After their jam session ends,
Todd walks me out
to the parking lot.

Mom waits
in the car, watching as
Todd waves to me before going
back inside the school.

Who is that?
Mom asks
as I put on my seatbelt.

Todd McPherson.
He's in APUSH with me.

Oh?

Mom's eyes twinkle
like sequins catching the light of a chandelier.

I think: Prom 1993
the emerald dress
her ruby lips.

Then something
       a memory
       a thought
douses the light in her eyes.

Promise me, Esme,
she says,
*that you won't fall too hard
for this boy?*

I don't know
what to say.
I'm not sure I have a choice
about how hard I fall.

Mom adds,
*I'm just saying
you have your whole life
ahead of you.*

We drive home
in silence.
I don't say anything, but
Mom's comment makes me wonder
if she regrets
falling too hard
for Dad.

MORE THINGS I DON'T SAY

Hey, Pumpkin,
Dad says
when I poke my head in.

The dog chair
smells like flowers.
I think Grammy Jean
has sprayed it with Febreze.

Dad showered, too.
His hair is combed,
his face pink.

What've you
been up to? he asks.

Just hanging out
with friends.

Mia?

No, some other friends
from school.
This girl named Zoe.

For some reason,
I don't say Todd's name.

She's in a band,
and I listened to some of their set.
They played Jim Croce.

I don't say,
When they played
I thought of you.
And I thought of Grampa Tom,
even though I never met him.

Oh yeah? They any good?

I say, *Yeah. Pretty good.*

CONVERSATION I OVERHEAR #3

Mom and Grammy Jean
talk in whispers
in the kitchen
after dinner.

Grammy Jean says
*I found a lawyer,
a* pro bono *one.
When I told her
about John's accident,
how he's waited for weeks
lying in that awful chair, in pain,
for the workers' comp to be approved
the woman   the lawyer
said she'd make a phone call.*

Grammy Jean
gets it out all in one breath.

I hear a cabinet door
slam shut.

Mom's voice bristles,
*Are you
SURE
this is free?*

And then with a hiss,
Did you give them a credit card?

Grammy Jean says,
I didn't give them anything,
except the facts.
Grammy's voice is soft soft.
Listen to me.
They just want to help.

No one just wants to help.

Let's see what happens.
It can't hurt, Grammy Jean
says, like she's trying to lure
a stray cat to eat the food she's put out.

My mother, gone astray,
so untrusting.
Even someone
trying to help.

When I was little
she'd tell me that
there was no shame
in asking for help.

At school,
                    at dance class,
if there was something
I didn't understand,
or couldn't do on my own,
there was nothing wrong
with speaking up.

Now she is lost
in a world where suspicion
blooms in place of trust.

She is all fear
and claws.

A GIRL AT MIA'S SCHOOL

On Thursday night
after dance class
I eat dinner over at Mia's.

Her mom asks about
        Grammy Jean's visit.
Her dad asks about
        school.
I don't go into many details—
just say that both are good.

Costume fittings this weekend!
Mia's mom says.
You girls must be excited about that?

Mia answers,
*Hopefully there's nothing
too weird this year.*

I think (to myself)
Hopefully everything fits.

Later in her room
I confess that I'm dreading
costume fittings.

Mia understands.
She's witnessed my
humiliation over the years.
She says,
*A girl at my school
had breast reduction surgery.
She said it wasn't too bad.
She looks great.*

Mia adds quickly,
I mean,
she seems happy she did it.

I never told Mia
my secret plans.
how I think I want
reduction mammoplasty
how I looked it up
when I was worried my
boobs would just keep growing
forever.

I can't tell if Mia
thinks I should do it.
I don't want to ask her
what she thinks.

> I'm too afraid she will say
> *You should.*
>
> Or maybe I'm more afraid she'll say
> *You shouldn't.*

MORE SURGERY THOUGHTS

That night
I lie awake thinking
about surgery again.

It sounded scary
when I looked it up.
I remember the words,
> *Like all surgeries,*
> *breast reduction surgery*
> *carries with it the risk of death.*

I think about Dad
        and his surgery.
But, for him,
it's different.
If he doesn't have surgery
he may never
live a normal life again.

Breast reduction surgery?

It makes me wonder
if a smaller chest
is worth dying for.

But mostly I wonder
if a smaller chest
will help me live
a better life.

FITTINGS

The costumes drape
from rolling racks
positioned around the studio floor.

In shades of purples,
greens and blues,
reds and pinks, and
white and black, like the never-ending
scarf of a magician.

Taped to the mirror,
costume photos cut from catalogues
form a collage that
look like some
fashion magazine
puked up pages
of beautiful, and
sometimes strange, designs.

Every dance number
has its own costume
and every class performs
three or four numbers.

The photos are arranged
by class. Everyone
ooohs and *ahhhs* at the pictures
in between
trying on sample costumes
to help us order the right size.

Only for me, there
is rarely a right size.

I know which one
will cause trouble:
the red one with the
three quarter sleeves and
slanted hem line skirt.
That would all be fine,
if not for the faux black leather vest
with seven silver snaps.

When I try it on,
just as I suspected,
there is no way those
snaps will close.

I go up and up
and up in size,
trying to get the vest
to fit
until the red skirt
bags out around me
like a tent.

Miss Regina comes over
to inspect the baggy bottom
and the vest which
still
will not stay closed.

Mia sneaks me
a look of sympathy.

Brooke wears a smirk.

*I guess Esme
will have to be cut
from that number,*
Brooke says.

Miss Regina glares
at Brooke,
but she does not disagree.

KENDALL SPEAKS UP

How about this one instead?
Kendall is looking at the costume photos.

I mean, not to be rude or anything,
Miss Regina, but
none of us like that pleather vest anyway.
This one is way more
badass.

Miss Regina walks over to Kendall,
cocks her head at the photo.

Badass, huh?
Miss Regina asks
with a sly grin.

Yeah,
Kendall says
with a grin to match.

I know the one she means.
It's red—
with a black mesh top
over a tank.
Definitely more stretch.

Okay, I'll call tomorrow
and make the switch.

Brooke rolls her eyes.

My face burns.

Kendall winks at me.

151

THANKSGIVING

We wake up early
to gently falling snowflakes.
Hushed preparations.
Oven heat warms the house, and
steam fogs the kitchen windows.

Mom and Grammy laugh
at onions that make them cry.
I bring Dad coffee.
Thanksgiving turkey reminds
all of us what love smells like.

Grammy lights candles.
Mom stirs stuffing, and gravy
bubbles on the stove.
I mash potatoes with cream.
Grammy sings Amazing Grace.

Platters and dishes,
steaming bowls crowd our table.
Somehow Mom managed
to deliver a whole feast
on a waitress salary.

Dad leans on the wall
smiling at the three of us
even in his pain.
He stays standing through dinner
and while having pumpkin pie.

Sitting upright is
unthinkable, even now.
But Dad insisted
on having this meal with us.
Fifteen weeks, he's been hurting.

When Grammy's phone rings,
we ask, *Who is calling now?*
Listening through tears,
she whispers, *It's the lawyer.*
We can plan the surgery.

ONE MORE THING

The next morning
Mom stares into space
at the kitchen table
both hands wrapped around her coffee mug.

I'm afraid to ask.

The folded piece of paper
grows creased and wrinkled
in the heat of my hand.

It's just a question.

And the answer
to any unasked question
is always no.

So . . .

I slide the printout
toward Mom.

I tell her how I've
found this breast specialist online.
I like her.
I want to go see her.

Mom looks at me
like I've asked
to go to the moon.
She unfolds the page,
and glances at the
doctor's bio.

When I read what the doctor wrote
about guiding each patient
to the decision that is right for them,
my breath caught in my chest
the words blurred
beneath tears I
didn't fully understand.

I think I know what's right for me.
A smaller chest would make life

                       easier.

But maybe I still need
a guide.
Maybe this doctor can help.

I just want to
talk to her.

But Mom
folds the paper

                  closed
folds her eyes

                  closed
shakes her head
to show her mind is

                  closed
Esme,
I can't.
I can't
take
on
one
more
thing.

MOM DOESN'T KNOW

what it's like
to carry around these boobs
      to try to dance
      or go to school
      or out in public
under the weight of them.

Mom (whose average breasts
stay safely tucked away)
doesn't know
what it's like
to ignore the stares of men—
grown men sometimes—
or maybe worse—
grown women.

Mom doesn't know
what it's like
to be ogled
to feel eyes
on a part of you
you cannot hide,
that invites the world
to stare.

SURGERY SCHEDULED

Dad's surgery is
scheduled for December 23rd.

It is the soonest
they can squeeze him in.

We take it, even though it means
he'll be in the hospital on Christmas.

An early Christmas gift,
Grammy Jean says.

I'm both
scared and relieved.
Surgery is the thing
that will bring Dad back
to us, help him walk
and work and sit at the kitchen table
again.

There may be a risk of death,
but we know surgery
is the only thing
that can give him back his life.

BA-BOOM

At our next dance class
Mia and I are determined to
get back on track
with Miss Regina.

The team works on our
contemporary number,
which involves a lot of leaps.

I chassé
                    step together
sink
down into my plié
                    and power off my front foot
squaring my hips and
raising my arms   like wings.
It's a good leap
solid technique and really great height.
I'm proud of it.

Until
in a pause in the routine
Brooke walks past and says low

BA-BOOM
                    BA-BOOM
                                        BA-BOOM.

And I know
that she means the bouncing
the upswing
and downswing of my boobs.

Only a few girls hear.

Kendall shakes her head.
Just ignore her.
She's still pissed about
Jane losing her spot.

But when we run it again,
I feel like everyone is watching my chest
thinking   BA-BOOM   BA-BOOM   BA-BOOM
I keep my plié shallow
too shallow to get any power
any lift.

Without power

              the leap is low
              half-hearted
              disappointing.

And I catch Miss Regina
shaking her head.

PAST DUE

On the way out
I spy the sign on the studio wall:

Costume payments
are due at this time.
Orders
will not be placed
without a deposit.

I don't know
how we will pay
the deposit.

I only know
without costumes
I can't dance.

MIA LEAVES FOR BERMUDA

in just two days.

In her basement
we breathe hard from our workout
and stretch.

We won't see each other again before Christmas.
I pull her gift from my bag.

When she opens the little box of beaded earrings,
she squeals, *Oh these are so cute!*
I knew she'd like them—a craft fair treasure
I found with Grammy Jean.
Only five dollars but they sparkle
in Mia's favorite colors: blue and orange.

She hands me my gift.
When I hold the box
in my hand, feel the heft of it,
I think I know what it is.

I open it:

> *Love*
> the perfume.

Oh Mia.

I know it's more than we agreed to spend.
But I really wanted you to have it.

We hug
even though
we're sweaty.

Mia tells me
she's going to be on the lookout
for cute boys
in Bermuda.

We wish each other Merry Christmas.
But for some reason I don't tell her
       about Dad's surgery, the way I haven't said anything
       about my costume deposit still unpaid
       about Mom not wanting to bring me to the breast surgeon.

Instead, I tell her
Text me some pics!
I'll miss you.

I hug my best friend.
She is excited to go,
but I want her to stay.

SURGERY DAY

I do homework on the carpet
of the hospital room
where we wait.

It's a special waiting room
on the same floor
as the operating room.
And we three—Mom, me, and Grammy Jean—
are the only people here.

Mom flips through magazines
looking at the pages
without reading.

Grammy Jean whispers she'll be right back
and steps out to go to the restroom.

Esme.

I look up.

Mom clutches a magazine to her chest.

What I said before
that day in the car
about not falling too hard . . .

I want you to know
      I don't regret
            falling.

Everything good in my life
is because I fell in love
with your dad.

*You're a smart girl
with a good heart.
Just trust it.*

*That's all
I'm saying.
Trust your heart.*

AFTER SIX HOURS

The doctor comes in.

Mom drops her magazine.

I jump up from the floor
and scramble to sit
next to Grammy Jean.

I don't know which of us
reaches for the other's hand first.
All I know is that
my hand locks with Grammy's.

The surgery went well.

I hear Mom breathe.

The doctor talks about
the long road ahead
      a rehabilitation facility
          physical therapy.

When he leaves,
I notice that
Mom holds tight
to Grammy Jean's other hand.

They lean their heads
together.
And Grammy whispers,
It's going to be
okay now.

CHRISTMAS

On Christmas morning
Mom texts from the hospital
sending a photo:
Dad sitting up straight—SITTING!
smiling in a Santa hat.

Merry Christmas, Love!
Dad's feeling pretty good now.
Can't wait to see you!
I reply with lots of hearts.
Grammy and I leaving soon!

When I was a kid
nothing was more magical
than Christmas morning.
My parents made sure of that,
under the tree, mounds of gifts.

Now, I wonder how they
managed it, all those presents.
This year, we've kept it
small, just a couple things each.
It all fits in two tote bags.

But, before we go,
Grammy hands me one box wrapped
in sparkly paper.
You should open this one now.
(Is it what I think it is?)

I tear it open
and yes—the gorgeous sweater,
soft as a kitten,
blue angora, I tried on
with her while we were shopping.

Grammy, I love it
but—she knows what I'm thinking
and puts up her hand.
We won't mention the price tag.
I had a coupon. She winks.

When I put it on,
the sweater wraps around me
not too tight, perfect
making me feel beautiful
and that's just what Grammy says.

THE BEST THINGS

At the hospital,
I plug in the tabletop tree
and we open gifts around Dad's bed
which does not smell like dog.

New garden gloves and some seed packets for Mom
an electric razor for Dad
a pair of big earrings for Grammy
new dance shorts for me.

Mom is so happy
she compliments my sweater
and doesn't even mention what it
must have cost. She says,
*That shade of blue reminds me
of the sky after a storm.*

Together, we watch Christmas movies
on the little TV
and eat some of the sugar cookies
we brought for the nurses.

When Dad's eyes droop,
Grammy Jean and I give our hugs
and head home
leaving Mom to stay

the night again, sleeping
on the little foldout chair
next to Dad's bed.

At home, Grammy Jean and I
watch *White Christmas*
and eat popcorn
and Hershey Kisses from my stocking.

Dancing is timeless
because OMG
Danny Kaye and
that tiny blond lady?
AMAZING!

We rewind
and watch
"The Best Things
Happen While
You're Dancing"
three times.

On the fourth time
Grammy Jean
pulls me to my feet,
and we
dance and laugh.
She twirls me
          dips me.
We dance.
And it is
the best thing.

THE BEST GIFT

When the movie ends,
Grammy Jean snores softly
on the couch next to me.

I click off the TV
and the room goes dark,
except for a soft glow from
the Christmas tree lights.

I wonder if Mom and Dad
are asleep too, if the little
tree in the hospital room
is still glowing, too.

It was a good day.
The nurses even had Dad
on his feet and walking.
It looked painful, but
Dad said it was a different kind
of pain.

Grammy Jean was right:
the best gift this Christmas
was Dad's surgery.
I sit a while longer
while Grammy Jean sleeps
and enjoy the quiet glow of the lights.

GHOSTS OF CHRISTMAS PAST

When I give Grammy Jean
a gentle shake to wake her
she stirs and whispers,
Tom?

I keep my hand on her shoulder.
Grammy, you should head to bed.

Her eyes blink open.
She places a hand on my cheek,
Esme, honey.
Merry Christmas, darling.

When I help her get up
from the couch,
she pulls me to her
for a long hug
and shuffles down the hall.

Grampa Tom's been gone
all those years
and she still
dreams of him.

A DATE

I've been dreaming—
or maybe daydreaming—of Todd.
As if on cue, he calls
to invite me to the movies, as in

AN ACTUAL DATE!
My first real date.

I text Mia, still in Bermuda,
to tell her I'm going   ON A DATE!

A DATE!

She texts back
a million heart emojis
and:
      I want ALL the details
      when I get back!
and then sends a photo
of her in her new bikini
by the hotel pool.

      The lifeguard here is really cute.

I zoom in to see
the dark-haired
bare-chested and muscled
boy in the background.
He's obviously watching Mia
who looks as amazing in the Bermuda sun
as she did under those dressing room lights.

When I tell Grammy Jean
I have a date,
she grins and with a far-off look says,
Ah Love.

A RIDE

Last year
when I was a freshman,
Tyler Burkett—
      football captain
      a senior
      with sparkling blue eyes—
invited me to
      go for a ride
           in his car.

I'd been waiting for Mom
to pick me up
from Key Club after school.

He was walking past and just stopped
where I was standing
with a group of girls.

He looked me over
delivered his trademark dazzling smile
and jutting his chiseled chin at me, said,
      Hey (he didn't know my name)
      want to go for a ride?

The girls
around me thought
I was crazy
when I said,
No thanks. My ride's coming.

But I saw how he looked at me.
I've been on guard since
seventh grade   when my boobs got big
and guys started to notice   make comments.
As if having these boobs
makes me   fast   slutty.

That wasn't dinner
        and a movie.
He wanted a ride.

He wasn't used to being turned down.
And he never asked again.

COWS AND MOVIES

Todd is the first boy
to ask me on a real date.
And I know he is interested in me
        not just my boobs.

Grammy Jean turns down the
music in the car.

You like this boy?
she asks as we pull into the movie theater parking lot.

I nod.

Listen to me,
no one ever bought the cow,
if they got the milk for free.

I can't help it.
        I laugh.
I haven't even had my first kiss!
And Grammy's worried about milk!

Grammy, it's just a movie.
And it's just Todd
who isn't like that.
And I'm not a cow.

She laughs back.
I know.
But you are my granddaughter. I just don't want to see you get hurt.

She kisses me on my forehead
and I step out of the car.

ARMREST

The armrest

at the movies is
both boundary
and bridge.

Shared territory.

During the movie,
my elbow sits on the armrest
between me and Todd.

Then his arm is there, too.

His pinky loops my pinky.
And the rest of our fingers join in,
linking together.

Holding hands
feels like we've crossed
some bridge
into new territory.

WANTING

When the movie is over
we step from the heated lobby
to the brisk air outside.
The winter sun sinks down,
as scheduled, at four p.m.

We stand next to the theater
on the sidewalk,
half lit by the outdoor lights.

Would you rather wait inside?
Todd thumbs toward the glass doors.
Todd's mom is on her way.
Grammy Jean, too.

My scarf hangs from my neck,
and Todd picks up the ends
and wraps them around my neck and shoulders.

He tucks the scarf under my chin
and smiles at me.
He's looking at my lips,
even though I'm not wearing
Love That Red.

Then he leans in
his face so close
his breath warm.

I close my eyes
and feel the soft
press of his lips
landing on mine.

177

Only . . .

a little off center
a kiss that seems to miss

dusting the corner
of my mouth
my cheek.

A first kiss
half kiss.

Hope that was okay.

I nod and open my eyes
whisper, *Yes.*

Todd McPherson has light brown eyes
so light they are almost green.
And he might be even smarter
than I thought.

Maybe he knows that
by giving me half a kiss,
he's left me
wanting the rest.

THE END OF CHRISTMAS BREAK

Grammy Jean has made a quiche
for dinner.

Mom looks tired after
a long day of getting
Dad settled in the rehab facility
where he'll be for the next three weeks.
Getting stronger.

I carry our dishes
set them in the sink

and the piece of mail on the counter
half-buried under the grocery flyer
catches my eye.

FREE TO ALL

If money is a wall
there should be things that are
   free to all

Things like
   kindness
      love
         hope and peace

And also things like:
   food
      shelter
        heat and light

But in the real world
   almost everything comes at a cost.

The electric bill
half-hidden on the counter
carries a warning
in red ink:

YOUR ACCOUNT IS PAST DUE.
IF PAYMENT IS NOT RECEIVED IN 30 DAYS,
YOUR ACCOUNT WILL BE SUSPENDED.

And just when I think
things are looking brighter
I imagine
our world
   DARK
our worries
   DARKER.

BACK TO SCHOOL

On my first day back
after break, I wear
my new sweater.

When I walk into Chemistry
I am greeted by the same shade of greyish-blue sky
leaning over our lab table.

Celine looks up
and I watch her face
as it registers that we are wearing
the same sweater.

OMG—nice sweater!

I laugh. *You too.*
We have good taste.

No doubt, mine is
a larger size
and I wait for Celine to say something.
About our differences.

But instead she just says,
Damn, we look hot!

She lights the Bunsen burner,
no longer afraid of it,
and we get to work.

GRAMMY JEAN TO THE RESCUE

When Grammy Jean
picks me up from school,
I plunk into the passenger seat.

I'm finishing a text to Todd
when I notice
we haven't moved.

Grammy Jean holds up
a folded piece of paper,
creased and wrinkled.

She hands it to me.
I don't need to open it
to know what it is.

Listen to me, Esme.
You know
I think you are perfect
just the way you are.
But it's smart
to get all the information.

She leans in
puts a hand on my arm.
Do you want to go?

I open the page.
Reread the information
about Dr. Nadia Lewis,
Plastic Surgeon,
Breast Care Specialist.

Yes, I say.

Good.
I booked an appointment
two weeks from today.

FIVE MONTHS

It's been five months
since we started on Elite
and Brooke is still angry.

The other Elite girls
have moved on
or lost interest.

Some, like Kendall
and Sofia, have actually started
to like us.

But Queen Bitchiness
hangs onto the grudge
the way some dancers
maintain the extension
on a leg hold,
toes arched above the head
steady.

The Queen is nothing
if not steady. So steady
she's predictable.

Predictable when she
jabs an elbow
in my ribs
while we line up.

I'm steady, too.
I don't flinch.

Brooke doesn't bother Mia.
She doesn't have to.

184

Tonight, Mia can't seem
to keep the timing tight
to keep her steps from stuttering.

I stay up on my feet
and work hard at convincing myself
I am good enough
to be here.

THE REASON WHY

After class
we step outside
into a frosty, clear night.

Kendall, in her army jacket,
calls *See you guys*
over the jingle of her keys.

And Sofia says, *See you tomorrow,*
to Mia.

Our alliances have worked.

I turn to Mia, but
my excitement melts.

I want to say,
our plan is working,
but Mia's eyes glint with tears.

I rush to say,
Things are getting better,
while Mia's eyes squeeze shut.

Her hands clench the strap of her bag.
It's not that, she says.
It's my knee.

DANCING THROUGH PAIN

Every dancer
dances through pain
at some point.
The trick is knowing
when not to.

It turns out Mia's knee
has been getting worse,
but she didn't say anything.

Just kept dancing through the pain.

I get it.

We've been working
hard

leaping and landing
hard

spinning and turning
and taking off
hard.

We've given everything
to this team
that wanted nothing
to do with us.

And now that we
are making progress,
Mia's knee
is giving up.

NOT EVEN A DISNEY HEROINE

That weekend,
I sleep over at Mia's.

She had an MRI
and her doctor told her
no dancing.
Four weeks of rest.

We both know
this means
she might miss
the first competition.

In Mia's room,
we click through
movies trying to find
the perfect one to distract.

None of them fit right.

The feel-good movies
        feel too good.
The sad ones
        might drag us under.
And the ones about
chasing down a dream
and catching it?
        Well, it's complicated

I want to say some
magical thing
to lift my best friend's spirits,
words to support and encourage.
Maybe you're just like all these
heroines that defy expectations.
There's always a dream,
and then a setback to overcome.
This is your setback,
I tell her.
Now you just need to
overcome it.

But Mia's face closes off,
a mix of annoyance and anger,
as she adjusts the ice pack
on her knee.

This isn't some movie, Esme.
I worked my knee too hard
           and now it may never be right.

I stay quiet
because it almost sounds like
there's blame in her words.
Does she blame me
           for working too hard
           for all the added practice times?

We watch
Black Panther,
and it makes me even sadder,
makes me miss my dad
who won't be home for
two more weeks,
and makes me miss
Chadwick Boseman, too.

Then we turn off the lights
both of us lying in the dark
wide awake
with our own thoughts.

For the first time
ever
in the history of us
we have nothing to say.

HOLDING THE SPACE

Miss Regina is not happy
about Mia's knee.

I see her talking with Mia
in the hallway,
giving her a lecture
even though
it's obvious that Mia pushed
herself because Miss Regina
was pushing us.

Once class begins,
Mia sits in a chair
in the corner of the studio
to watch.

The rest of us
hold the space
where she would be in the routine.

We must imagine
her there,
imagine Mia
occupying
time and space,
in the place
where she should be.

Miss Regina keeps
calling out,
Hold the space, girls.
Hold the space!

We try,
but it's not the same.

COLD THAT BITES

We are already outside,
in the parking lot,
when I see Mom's text about
running late, still at the restaurant.
A chimichanga emergency, maybe.

The January wind bites at
the glimpses of skin we have exposed.

You have it easy,
Mia says to me
from out of nowhere.

And I don't know
what she means.

What?

*If you have surgery,
it's over and done with.
Breast reduction
is simple,
compared to knee surgery.*

*Who said anything
about surgery?* I ask.

*My doctor says
I'll need it.
If I want to keep dancing.
The knee can't take it.*

The cold feels brisk,
cooling me down
after the heat of dancing.
But Mia's been sitting all class.
She tucks her chin
deeper into her North Face.

What will you do? I ask.

She shrugs and doesn't look at me.

*If I have surgery now,
I'll be out for the rest of the season.
I don't know.
Maybe the summer.*

Ice forms on the edges
of Mia's words, making them
biting and sharp.

Is she angry at
Miss Regina?
At me?
Does she blame me
for her needing surgery?

And what does that have
to do with breast reduction surgery?
I haven't even told her about the
appointment Grammy made.

I tell myself
she's still my best friend,
and none of this
is easy.

I tell myself,
she's cold,
and Mom won't be here
for another fifteen minutes,
but I don't offer to go back inside.

WEDNESDAYS ALONE

I start going to the studio
after school
on Wednesdays.
Alone.

Even if Mia was allowed
to dance right now,
she couldn't
join me. Her school is
too far away.

At this time of day
two p.m.
the studio is quiet—
no screech of little voices
no endless chatter
no rumors
no gossip
no words that bite.

It is church quiet.

At first, I don't even
play music
just stretch and move
in the silence.

I know I should be
working on my technique
and I will
but just for a little while
I let go of *should*.

I put in my earbuds
and let the beat
power me.

Without anyone watching
without any eyes to judge
my body warms, loosens,
moves the way
a memory can bring a smile
to your lips.

I am jumping and leaping
and remembering all the reasons
I love to dance.

RECOVERY

Just like the surgeon said
Dad's recovery is a long journey,
a long journey down
sterile white hallways
with faded watercolor art
in frames screwed into the wall.

Down those halls
Dad shuffles with his walker,
gripping the handles
breathing hard and
sweating,
a full-body workout
pain included.

At first Dad talked about his
physical therapist, Rudy,
as if he was in prison
and Rudy was the warden.

But later Dad talks about Rudy
like he's a demigod.

Because somehow Dad has gone
from wheelchair to walker
with hopes of
walking on his own.

Because somehow Rudy
has worked a miracle.

ANOTHER MIRACLE

After class
Miss Regina calls,
Esme, can I see you please?

And I know this it.
I'm being cut from the team.

Today's class was okay,
better than it has been.
But there's no hiding that
I'm hesitant, still off.

I keep my eyes on the floor
as I walk to Miss Regina.

I don't know if you knew,
she begins, *but the bill for your*
costumes was overdue?
And your spring tuition?

I nod, and my eyes well.

I open my mouth hoping
words and maybe a solution
will come out.

Luckily, they were just taken care of.
Miss Regina smiles.
You're all set.

My face must reflect
the effort of trying to piece together
the puzzle of
Miss Regina's words
because she adds,
It's been paid.
Costumes and your tuition balance, as well.

What? I don't understand.

We got an
anonymous donation.
I should feel like a weight has been lifted.
And I do.
I'm still on the team.
And I'm no longer "overdue."

Oh, okay,
I manage to say.
Miss Regina pats my shoulder
before walking away.

But something else pushes down on me
because I hate thinking that I owe someone something.

I gather my things
and wonder if maybe
Grammy Jean came to the rescue
with one of her credit cards?
Or maybe there really was an
anonymous donor?
Or maybe the studio
just waived the costs?

If I had to bet I'd say it was
the studio.
I've danced here forever.
They wouldn't just let me
drop because I couldn't pay.

Right?

198

DAD'S LAST DAY

On Dad's last day at the rehab facility
a small crowd has gathered
to send him off.

I meet Rudy
the demigod/physical therapist
for the first time.
His face, wrinkled and weathered,
looks human enough.
He's as old as Dad
maybe older.

But his arms, chest, and back
have the strength of a god.
Strong enough to lift
a fallen man
from the ground,
from his lowest point,
and set him right again.

Dad's eyes shine
as he shakes Rudy's hand.

Thanks, is all Dad
can manage.

You did the work,
Rudy replies.
Now keep going.

And he does.
Dad walks to the car
with only a cane.

DAD NEEDS THE CANE

for a little while longer.
Just to be extra safe.

But he doesn't need
the dog chair anymore.

My uncle Larry doesn't want
it back, either. He offered
to come by on the weekend
to help move it, but Mom
wants it out of the house
now.

Together, Mom and I
manage to drag it to the curb
for trash pickup.

Brushing her palms together,
Mom wipes away the doggy stink.

Good riddance,
she says.

But for just a moment
as we walk across the
front lawn, I look back
to see the chair on its side
at the curb.

I think how it served its purpose,
kept Dad almost comfortable
at a time when that was almost impossible.

I whisper
Thank you.

MIA IS M.I.A.

Mia's decided
she isn't
coming to class
if she can't dance.

We've texted a few times,
and she said
she won't come, even
for the little kids.

There's a lot that's been unsaid
between us
       my dad coming home
       my half-kiss with Todd
       getting an appointment with Dr. Lewis.
And if her knee was bothering her so much
       why didn't she just tell me?

If she had told me
       I wouldn't have pushed so much
       or added so many practices.

Then again—

       Maybe I should have noticed.

       Maybe I should have asked.

SATURDAY NIGHT STUDY BREAK

At Todd's house
Saturday night
we sit at the dining room table
our APUSH handouts spread out in front of us,
an intimidating feast.

His mom and dad
cook dinner
in the kitchen.
They seem happy
to have me over.

My back is aching,
after dance today,
and I'm wishing I took some ibuprofen
before I came over.

When Todd goes to get us some water,
I lean forward against the table
and rest my breasts
for just a minute.

When I hear his footsteps
I pull back.
The relief is gone,
but in its place
Todd's face leaning into mine
to hand me my glass.

KISSING

I am still waiting
for the second half
of my kiss with Todd.

I doubt it will happen
tonight, at his house
with his parents
right there.

A kiss is a very strange thing
when you think about it.

I mean who thought
it was a good idea
to press lips together
and then open mouths
and share tongues?

But looking at Todd's lips
I feel this
deep, ancient part of me
that instinctually
understands
a kiss
is not
so strange
after
all.

SWINGS

The next Wednesday,
on my walk from school
to the studio,
I notice two girls on the swings
on the elementary school playground.

They swing and talk.
They're too tall to be little kids.
And the elementary school doesn't let out
for another hour.

Then I realize
I know them.

I pull my hood up
because the February wind cuts through me
but also to hide my face.

Brooke
   and
     Jane

Jane, who lost her spot on Elite
Jane, who quit rather than go back to Juniors.

I keep walking,
through the realization that
Jane and Brooke
are friends
maybe even best friends.

My heart swings back and forth
        because I know
what it's like to have a best friend
        (at least I used to)
and I would have done
        just about anything
to help her.

GRAVITY AS NEMESIS

In the studio
I struggle.
I can't help but hear
HOW GOOD COULD YOU BE?
every time I turn or leap.

When I was six or seven
I started having this recurring dream
where I would lift off in a grand jeté

and sail away on a breeze
gliding on air
over treetops and buildings and roads.

Now, the air goes out
from under me
as soon as I push off.

My boobs
BA-BOOM
on my torso.

At some point
the dream just stopped.
Probably around the time
I stopped feeling weightless.

My bones are not hollow,
my flesh, too heavy.

The pull of gravity
tethers me to the earth.

The pull of gravity
my nemesis now

and the sky
out of reach.

FROM THE WAIST UP

In the exam room
my heart beats so loudly
I think Grammy Jean and the nurse
can hear it.

The nurse talks as she takes my blood pressure
and asks about my medical history.
She tells us her name is Sarah,
and she's worked with Dr. Lewis for eight years now.

When she tells me
I'm going to like Dr. Lewis,
I believe her.

Take off everything
from the waist up.

Sarah hands me a pale pink gown.
Then put this on so it
opens in the front.

She pulls the curtain
closed around the examination table.
Grammy Jean waits
in a chair on the other side.

I wriggle out of my hoodie
and my T-shirt and
finally, my bra.

The room is warm, overheated,
but I shiver when I pull the thin pink fabric around me
and fold my arms over my chest
      as if I could hold myself in
      as if the pink material could contain all of me.

DR. NADIA LEWIS

has perfect posture
and a normal-size chest
contained within her white doctor coat.

She wears her dark curls
pulled back
and her smile is wide.

She talks about breasts
like she's ordering
dinner at a restaurant.

I like her.
So when she asks,
I tell her about:

the aches in my neck
and shoulders
and back
the scabs from my sports bras
the feeling of being off
being weighed down
when I dance.

How dance costumes don't fit right.
How nothing really fits right.

I stick to the physical stuff.

I don't say
how much it bothers me
when people stare.

How they judge me
even though they don't know me,
like I must be a slut
or whatever.

Not just boys
but men.
And not just men
but women.

As though
having this chest
makes me
a sexual thing.

As though
having this chest
was a choice I made
instead of something
I live with.

AFTER TALKING

She asks if she can examine me.
She draws the curtain mostly closed,
leaving Grammy Jean on the outer edge again.

I lay back on the table
and stare up at the ceiling
as she opens the gown.
She talks about breast cancer and self-exams
as her fingers pad in circles
around the flesh of me.

She asks me to sit up.
I look away,
focusing intently
on a poster of breast tissue
on the wall.

It's a cross-section
labeled with little arrows:
Mammary nodes
Lobes
Suspensory ligaments
Lactiferous ducts

I read about the
Signs and Symptoms of Breast Cancer
and think about how no one has seen
my naked breasts
ever.

Not Mom—at least not for years.

Not Mia.

Just me
and now, Dr. Lewis.

TALL

After the exam, Dr. Lewis
covers me back up and
asks me to stand.

I tie the pink strings of the gown
thankful for even the thin coverage.

Dr. Lewis pulls the curtain back,
and Grammy Jean meets my eyes.
Without words, she
asks if I'm okay.

I nod in reply.

Then Dr. Lewis comes behind me,
one hand lands lightly on each shoulder,
and she pulls back
gently.

Dr. Lewis says:
I want you to think
TALL.

From now on
no slouching
no letting your chest sink in.

Dr. Lewis says:
Shoulders back.
Spine strong.
TALL
Like there is a cord
running through the center of you
pulling you upward.

*If you do nothing else
maintain good posture.*

Dr. Lewis says:
*When you catch yourself slouching
or sinking into yourself
think
TALL.*

I wait for her to offer
a cure, to say
SURGERY.

But she doesn't.

What she offers
sounds too easy.

I'm not sure just thinking
TALL
will lift the weight of the world
off my chest.

GRAMMY JEAN ASKS

Maybe Grammy Jean
has doubts about thinking TALL, too,
because she asks,
*If Esme decides
she wants surgery
will insurance cover it?*

*Well, that's a bit
complicated,*
Dr. Lewis admits.

*In order for surgery to be covered
we'd need to establish a medical necessity.*

*We'd have to demonstrate
some kind of physical, medical problem
caused by the size of Esme's breasts.*

Dr. Lewis pauses,
and I think how
this is just like Dad's surgery.

He needed the surgery
but no one believed him.

Even necessity
bangs its head against
the money wall.

Then Dr. Lewis says,
*But we may be
getting ahead of ourselves.*

THE OTHER THING

Dr. Lewis looks between
Grammy Jean and me.
*The other thing
you need to do
is invest in good quality bras.*

*Bras that offer better support
than what you've been wearing.
Thicker, cushioned straps.*

*We want to stop those grooves
from getting any more pronounced.
Let the scabbing heal.*

She gives me a handout
about breast care
and points to the bottom of the page:
a list of websites
that sell high quality
(aka expensive) bras.

Now, let's do this,
she says.

*You get yourself
some better bras
and you keep thinking
TALL.*

When she says the word
her own back straightens,
her chest and her chin lift.

I sit up
try to feel the pull
of that imaginary cord.

We'll give it another
six months or so.
Once we're sure
your breasts have stopped growing,
we can talk about our options.
Surgery is one option,
but it's not right for everyone.

My heart sinks.
Six more months
          and even then
          who knows if the surgery
          would be approved.

Dr. Lewis tries to meet
my eyes.
Let's see how the bras work out
and the good posture,
and then we'll talk.
Okay?

Okay, I say.
But I'm not sure it is.

CREDIT CARDS AREN'T JUST FOR A LITTLE FUN

In the car
Grammy Jean
dabs at her eyes
with a tissue.

Grammy, I'm okay. Really.

I know you are, honey.

Then she opens her purse
and pulls out a silver credit card.

Listen to me,
as soon as we get home
you take this and
you log into those sites
and you order yourself
six new bras and
two new sports bras.

But Grammy . . .

Now, Esme
Don't you argue with me.

And the way
she says it
I know she is serious.

She pulls me to her
even though the gear shift
is between us.

A kiss planted in my hair
an earring tangled
Beautiful
     Beautiful
          Esme.

CONVERSATION I OVERHEAR #4

Back at home,
Mom and Grammy Jean
are in the kitchen.

*So, I took Esme
to see that doctor.*

>*You did what?
>Jean, you had no—*

Have you seen her shoulders?

>*What do you mean?*

*The girl has scabs
from her bra straps.*
Grammy Jean's voice cracks.

Mom's soft whisper
fills the empty air,
>*What?*

*Listen to me.
Esme is smart
and strong and
has a good heart.
You've raised her well.*

*She needs
to have all the information
so she can make the choice
that is best for her.*

Then
a sniff
a rustle of fabric

an embrace
and whispered words,
It's okay. She's okay.
She's going to be okay.

WITHOUT MIA

Wednesday nights
with the little kids
are almost worse than
Tuesday or Thursday nights with the team
because
the little kids miss her, too.

They ask
the same questions I have.

Is Miss Mia okay?
they ask.

Is her knee getting better?
they ask.

When will Miss Mia be back?
they ask.

And I can only answer,
I don't know.

She's not responding
to my texts.

BOWLING

I can't remember the last time
I went bowling
but Todd asked me to go
with him and Zoe and Owen
on Friday night.

We rent shoes
and get settled in our lane.

As Todd helps me pick a ball,
his body curves into mine,
his hand on my shoulder,
our faces close as he explains
something about physics
but I'm more interested
in the curve of his eyebrows
and the softness of his lips
than physics or bowling.

I still want the rest
of that kiss.

My first few tries aren't bad.
At least I keep the ball out of the gutter.

Zoe and I want nachos
and head to the snack bar
midway through the game.

We notice two guys
watching us.
They're older than high school,
maybe in college, and
the way they look at us
tells me they're not keeping
anything, especially their minds,
out of the gutter.

We try to ignore them.

One of them says
loud enough for us to hear,
This place has the best bowling balls.

The other guy laughs,
looks right at me.
*Yeah. We should come here
more often.*

Zoe is standing at my side,
Are they serious?
We glare at them
until they look away,
go back to playing.

Unbelievable, Zoe says.
We turn our backs,
and I am glad to have Zoe at my side.

It happens, I say.

It still sucks, Esme.

In that moment
I notice how my back
has rounded into
an armadillo shell,
my chest retreating
into it
braced against the words.

Maybe Dr. Lewis was right.
I feel again the gentle pull of
her hands on my shoulders
telling me to think TALL.

I try to find that inner cord
running through me and
straighten myself TALLER.

Yeah, I say as my back straightens
the world is full of . . .

I pause.
I know what I wanted to say
but my eyes travel down the end of
the shiny bowling lanes where
mechanical contraptions are setting
rows of pins back in place.

The world is full of . . . pinheads.

Pinheads?
Zoe asks.

Yeah, you know, not a lot going on up there.
I tap on my temple.

And Zoe's laugh is long
and loud, as beautiful
as her singing.

224

THINKING A THING

I do not know if
thinking a thing
makes it come true.

But all day long
      walking between classes in the hall
      in Chem, where Celine said I looked different
      even in gym class when I spiked the volleyball
I have been thinking TALL

and I swear
I have grown
a few inches.

FINE

Mia rejoins dance class this Saturday
after her month of rest.

And I'm nervous.
The fact that she stopped
responding to my texts
means she must be mad.
And I'm not sure how
to make this right.
How are you?
I ask her.

But all she says is
Fine.

How's the knee?

It's fine.

I'm about to say
I'm sorry, sorry
for pushing so hard.

I want to say
how much I missed her.

But then Mia bends over at the waist
tucking her head to her knees
like stretching
is the most important thing
in the world.

When Miss Regina claps
and orders us into position
everyone lines up
like nothing has changed

but everything has.

THINGS DON'T GO ACCORDING TO PLAN

At the break,
Mia talks with Soul Star Sofia.
They are smiling and
      laughing.
Maybe Mia is just sticking to our plan
to make allies.

But I know that's not it.
The way they talk with their
heads close together,
reminds me of how
we used to talk.

At the end of class,
as I slip my jazz shoes off,
I ask Mia
if she wants to do something
tomorrow.

She looks at me
and doesn't say anything.

*Maybe we can
catch up?* I offer.
It's been
over three weeks of us not
seeing each other.

I can't. I have plans.
She looks at her Apple Watch.

Sorry, Esme.
Mia walks out with Sofia.

228

MALL

The next day
I go to the mall with Todd
who needs a new pair of black pants
to wear for jazz band.
The ones he wore last year are
two inches too short.

I thought I was done growing
but who knows,
he says
which makes me think
about Dr. Lewis's comment
about my breasts and
making sure they've stopped growing.
And, oh PLEASE, let them be done growing.

Todd's mom gave him money for pants
and for us to get lunch.

After burritos at Chipotle
we find black pants
and a fun pair of black socks
with guitars on them.

We're in line at Starbucks
when Todd says,
Hey, isn't that your friend, Mia?

He points.
And I see Mia,
walking away from us.

229

I can tell it's her
with shopping bags
hanging from her arms.

She's with someone.
And even from behind
I can tell it is
Soul Star Sofia
who has bags to match.

FALLING BEHIND IN CHEMISTRY

Before class
I skim quickly
the lab instructions.

Wait,
Celine says
looking over my shoulder
You didn't do the reading?

I keep my eyes
trained on the page
and nod.

Between spending time with Todd
and extra hours at the studio
Chemistry hasn't been the priority.

Celine laughs.
I kind of love when you're not so nerdy.

We have not even started
the lab when we see Mr. Silva
walking toward us.

Celine sidles in close to me,
trains her eyes on the instructions, too.

When Mr. Silva clears his throat,
and asks if we were planning to get started,
Celine tucks her blond hair behind one ear.

231

Sorry, Mr. Silva,
she tilts her head and says,
I forgot to do the reading.
Esme was just giving me time to catch up.
She blinks at him innocently.

If she was a cartoon,
she'd be a doe or a kitten,
something adorable
with big eyes.

Her charms seem to work.

Okay, Mr. Silva says,
but let's get moving.
You don't want to
run out of time.

We stumble through
the lab together
and manage not to
light anything on fire or
blow up the classroom.

Turns out
even partners you don't choose
can work out for the best.

DANCE COMPETITION #1

EVERYTHING COULD BE DIFFERENT

In the dressing area,
when I put the tube
of *Love That Red*
to my lips,
I can't help but
think of Todd
who wanted to come today
but had his own trumpet audition.

Mom and Grammy Jean
are in the audience.

Dad stayed home.
He still has limitations.
He can't sit longer than one hour,
can't stand more than twenty minutes.

No way was he making
the two-hour car ride to get here,
never mind the auditorium seats all day.

I told Dad he wasn't missing much.
No solos or duets for me this year.

When I see my old Juniors teammates
laughing and talking and acting crazy
together while they do their makeup and hair,
I miss them.

Angie, who I still sit with
sometimes at lunch,
waves at me.
I wave back.

Mia is in the hallway with Sofia
taking pictures.
Their pointe
routine is coming up
and they are dressed in
soft lavender.
They'll have to fluff
the tulle of their tutus
after pressing together
for photos.

I think about Mia's text that day
in the backseat of her mother's car.
*Maybe we should
go back to Juniors.*
What if I had said yes?
What if we went back to our old team?

If we had,
everything would be different.

NUDE, NOT NUDE

Last year on Juniors
Mia and I were paired in a duet
that Miss Regina called STUNNING.

No longer a duo,
    (on or off the dance floor)
we blend into Elite,
two faded points of light
in a constellation of stars.

Now I just hope to
keep my balance and
keep my boobs
tucked inside the new
sports bra and spandex
leotard the color of my skin.

The new bras have
made a difference.
My shoulders are healing,
and my neck and back don't ache
the way they used to.

In the mirror backstage
between costume changes
I am nude, not nude,
just enough fabric
holding me together
cinching   compressing.

I remind myself
I don't dance
for praise
or prizes.

I dance for me
for that feeling of
being weightless
like at any minute
I'll lift off and fly away

      even though for a long time now
that's been
a faraway dream.

THE ELITE TWELVE (READY TO GO)

We are dressed,
for the first number
in our red with black mesh
looking badass.

On the way down the hall,
toward the stage,
I hear my name.

Esme.
Hey, Esme.
It's Brooke.

Then she's walking
next to me.

The other girls
are a few paces ahead.

Hey, I just wanted to say
good luck.
She smiles,
a *Love That Red* smile.

I look at her
with question-mark eyes.

Maybe this is her
saying sorry.

No, really,
she says.
Good luck
trying to keep those things
under control.

She cups her two hands
in front of her own
chest and shimmies her shoulders.
BA-BOOM   BA-BOOM   BA-BOOM!

She winks before
running off
to the front of the pack.

PACKING IT UP

After the competition,
Miss Regina tells us she's proud,
but that by the next competition
we'll need to step it up
even more.

Brooke wins Diamond for her solo.
Reagan and Alyssa win Ruby
      for their duo.
Mia's pointe class wins Sapphire.

When we are packing up, I ask Mia
How's your knee?

It's fine.

She doesn't even look up.

Most everyone else has cleared out.

Mia . . .

but I don't know what to say.
I want to ask
are we done being friends?
What's going on?

She looks up and shrugs.
I don't know.
I guess I'm just
    moving on.
She stuffs things in her duffel
and snaps her makeup case closed.

You know, she says
as she throws her duffel
over her shoulder,
*you were so focused
on working hard
you never even thought
about anything else.*

And I know for sure
she blames me for
her knee.

*And then, you never even said
thank you. You wouldn't even be
dancing if it weren't for me.*

And my mind spins
in a dizzying pirouette.

What?

*You never even said thank you.
          Who do you think paid for you?*

And I understand.

My costume bill.
My tuition.

The anonymous donor.
It wasn't the dance studio.

Of course,
it was Mia
          or really Mia's parents.

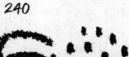

They're always doing things
for charity.

Mia shakes her head. Maybe she notices
the truth of it washing over me,
maybe she realizes I didn't know.
But she just walks out.

I realize this is
what I've become to her.

I am no longer the best friend.
I am the charity case
and I'm tired.
It's been a long day.

Between Brooke's teasing
and Mia's indifference
and now this . . .
I forgot all about
being
TALL.

WHEN WE GET HOME

The house is quiet
too quiet.

Then we hear a grunt.
Mom hasn't gotten her keys out of the door,
she leaves them in the lock,
and rushes in calling
John?

Grammy Jean follows
right behind Mom.
In the living room
Dad is on the floor.
I hear his raspy voice,
I don't . . . know what happened.
I couldn't grab my cane.
One minute I was up
      and next I was going down.

His head is bloody.
He must have hit the coffee table
on the way down.

Esme, Grammy Jean says,
call 911.

No, Dad argues.

We won't be able to lift you,
Mom says,
and you need to go to the hospital.

No, I'm fine.
Call Larry.
Dad's voice
sounds weak.

I dial 911.

IF A TREE FALLS

When the 911 operator asks
What's your emergency?
I hear myself answer,
sounding like a little girl,
My daddy fell.

I give our address
and go outside to the driveway
to wait for the ambulance.

And think about
that old question:
If a tree falls
in the forest and no one
is around to hear it,
does it make a sound?

And I decide
it doesn't matter.

If a tree falls
and no one is around,
the tree stays down.

SNOW DAY

Outside, the Monday morning world
is hushed and white,
a blank canvas,
a landscape starting over.

The house is hushed
too.
Mom and Dad are still in bed.
But I hear Grammy Jean
making tea in the kitchen.

The emergency room doctor
said Dad was okay.
Because he'd spent most of the day
on the floor, he was
dehydrated.
But no concussion.

He'll need to restart PT.

He was lucky, the doctor said.
I don't think Dad feels lucky,
because he's back to using a walker.

The school has already sent
an automated message
canceling due to inclement weather.

I will let this day
be a gift.
I have something I need
to write, but for a moment
I just stare out the window
watching a world washed in snow
and wondering how everything can change overnight.

245

WHERE DO BIRDS GO IN A STORM?

Caught in the swift and silent
rush of snow that threatens
to whip them away
in a torrent of wind

where do birds go?

Do they take cover
tucked deep within
an evergreen canopy?

Do they huddle together for warmth
knowing their survival depends
on each other?

Do they anchor themselves
to the rough bark of a branch,
hope that it holds steady,
and hold on for dear life?

As they shelter together,
do they pray to a little bird god
for the storm to pass,
for the sun to come out
so they can let go
lift off, and
fly free?

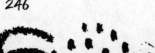

HOW TO WRITE A THANK-YOU NOTE

It's harder than you think
making words mean
what is in your heart.

I push aside any feelings,
a whole jumble of them,
I have about Mia.
I try to just think about
her parents.

Her parents
who I've known since I was four
who came to every birthday party
who fed me countless meals.

Her parents
who shared stories
who told jokes
while we drove to dance.

Her parents
paying for my dance tuition
for my costumes.

Without them I wouldn't be dancing.
It is that simple.

My pen hovers over the scrap piece of paper.
I don't dare to put the words
into a fancy card
until I get them right.

But I can't get them right
until I write them.

I google how to write a thank-you note:

    1. Express your thanks
    2. Keep it brief
    3. Explain how you will use the gift
       or what it meant to you.

I put the pen to paper
and say thank you
and try to tell them what it's meant:

It's been a hard few months
and even though dance has been hard, too,
without it,
       I would've been   lost.

I tell them I will never
forget their generosity
and the words on the page
spread to cover everything
that's in my heart.
I let what's inside me
      out.

By the end,
tears dot the paper
because I know

I may have lost Mia
as my best friend
but this gift
from her parents was given
not as a charity case.

It was a gift
given with love.

248

THE SNOW IS MELTING

It's early March
and Grammy Jean
needs to go back to Florida.

I've been away too long, she says.

She hands me a card
with my name
in her beautiful cursive
on the envelope.

Read this later.

*Now, remember,
when you start looking at colleges
you'll always have
free room and board
in central Florida, okay?*

She pulls me in for a hug,
my hair getting caught in her
big hoop earrings.

My beautiful,
        beautiful
                Esme.

Her whispered words
reverberate
through the whole of me.

AFTER WE DROP GRAMMY OFF

at the airport
the house has gone flat
like someone's let all the air out.

Alone in my room,
I open the card
and laugh out loud.

Another dimpled Dolly face
greets me. And, a Dolly quote:
*Find out who you are
and do it on purpose.*

Inside,
it's Grammy Jean's wisdom:

> *My dear Esme,*
>
> *Choices are
> stepping stones
> on a path. Each one
> brings you
> closer to one thing
> further away from
> something else.*
>
> *But you get to decide.
> You pick the next step.*
>
> *I am always here for you.*
>
> *And you should know
> that when I have choices*

that are mine to make,
I'll think WWMED?

What Would My Esme Do?

All my love,
Grammy Jean

SPAGHETTI AND MEATBALLS

When Todd is nervous
he chatters.
Not like teeth chattering.
I mean talking.
He talks
           a lot.

Mom offered to have
Todd over for dinner
I think to help fill
the hole that Grammy Jean
left behind.

While Mom dishes
      her famous meatballs
      and spaghetti, she asks Todd about school.
And Todd explains that he's in APUSH
with me but we're in different chemistry classes.
He lists his other classes and their teachers.
Mom nods along politely as we hand her plate
after plate to fill.

      Dad asks whether he plays sports.
      And Todd talks about marching band.

Dad nods while we sit around the table
      and Todd's voice fills every empty space
      which is way better than those
      long awkward silences that sometimes
      happen at dinners.

Mom goes to add a meatball
to Dad's plate and the meatball
rolls off the hill of pasta
onto the table with a splat
and then somersaults
toward the cliff
of the table edge.

I stare
and for the briefest
second, we're all quiet
waiting to see if the meatball
will go over.

It stops right at the edge.

That was close.
Dad laughs
and stabs the runaway meatball
with his fork
and adds it to his plate.

Yeah. Todd then laughs.
*For a minute I thought
it was going to be like
that song.*

Dad raises his eyebrows
and then
Todd
starts
singing

*On top of spaghetti
All covered with cheese*

He pauses for a second
but then goes on:
*I lost my poor meatball
When somebody sneezed.*

My parents stare at him
as Todd keeps going,
singing the story of
the meatball rolling
off the table and out the door.

Oh yeah, I remember that song,
my dad says
to my surprise.

And then
Mom chimes in,
*I always thought that song
was kind of gross.
I mean,
how big was that sneeze?*

And Dad laughs
and says, *Hey, that meatball
just wanted to have an adventure.*

Yeah. Todd smiles.
*A rolling meatball
gathers no sauce!*

Somehow this makes
everyone laugh.

And the rest of dinner
is filled with stories and laughter and
the eating of meatballs
before they can escape.

DANCE COMPETITION #2
MAYBE TODAY

I'll stand
TALL.

Mom
is here to cheer me on.

Dad is home,
with Uncle Larry.

I promised to send pics
to Grammy Jean.

So maybe today
I'll dance
for the love of it
for the thrill of competition
for the exhilaration of a stage
        lit up and glowing
        in a dark theater.

for that pause,
        that heartbeat of anticipation
        just before the music starts.

and when it does
        that rush of sound filling
        all the space where doubt used to be

for that feeling
        of taking off
        of letting go so you can soar.

Maybe today
I'll dance for that.

SURPRISE

I am in the dressing area,
ready to go even though
the first group number
is an hour away,
when I get Mom's text:
Come to the lobby.

And there is tall Todd McPherson
standing there,
holding a dozen red roses in his arms.

You came?

Surprise. These are for you.
Love That Red Roses.

I raise my eyebrows at him.

Well, that's what I call them.

He places them in my arms.

He is looking
at my *Love That Red* lips.

And before I can think,
I am up on my tiptoes
and leaning in,
claiming the other half of the kiss
that Todd owed me,
and then some.

THIS KISS

This kiss is
     warm
         and soft
            and slow.

I can smell the roses
I'm still holding and wonder
if this is what love smells like.

When we pull apart,
I see my mom and
Todd's mom standing there.

Todd's blush burns
out to the tips of his ears.

My whole face matches my lipstick.

Sorry, I say to Mom
and Mrs. M. when they
come closer.

Mom shakes her head
(and I think she kind of smiles)
and Mrs. M. waves her hand
in the air like she's swatting away a fly.

And Todd leans
down and whispers,
so only I can hear,
I'm not.

PHOTOS

One of Todd and
me, standing TALL
next to him,
our faces still pink
after our first (full) kiss,
a dozen roses in my arms.

Me and Kendall,
whose nose ring is out,
but still looks badass,
in our matching black mesh.

The Elite team
in our lyrical costumes,
pale, grey-blue.

Me and Mom,
her eyes smiling
our arms around each other
her cheek pressed to mine.

I send them all to Grammy Jean.

PRACTICALLY FLAWLESS

We file off stage
following our lyrical group number and
Miss Regina calls,
Nice job, girls.

I head back to the dressing area,
but Miss Regina
beckons to me,
and says,
Esme,
very nice.
Practically flawless.

The words wind
themselves inside me
through me
lifting me
making me TALL.

Most of the others
are already too far ahead
to have heard
but Brooke is just close enough.

She rolls her eyes.
But even her reaction
can't douse the light
inside me.

GOOD DAY

After my last costume change,
Faith walks by and sees my roses
Those roses are beautiful, Esme.

Thanks.
They're from my boyfriend.

And I realize it's the first time
I've called Todd my boyfriend.

The other Elite girls
notice the roses and
say things like,
    Lucky
        Wow
            Gorgeous

When Angie sees them,
she comes over.
Devon has never brought me roses.

The roses really are perfect,
each one a whorl of red velvet
nestled among dots of white
baby's breath and dark green
foliage, as beautiful
as Christmas lights.

I could stare at them all day.

But right now,
I've decided to go and
watch the pointe performance.

TRIUMPH

A bunch of us
have gathered to watch
the pointe routine, which is called
Triumph of Religion.

Sofia shines like
       the Soul Star she is.
And Mia is
       Small and Powerful
       and transcendent.

The dance is a triumph
of religion
if religion means
building a bridge between
reality and the ethereal or
believing in some greater power
that can lift you from earth and stage
and make you part of the heavens.

Mia's artistry
shines, from her long neck
to her fingertips that seem to reach
and hold the music
to her toe tips
touching down
in singular points
before lifting off.

The other dancers are
beautiful, but
Mia and Sofia
float across the stage
a matched pair
built for ballet
both
tiny
sinewy
narrow
lighter than birds.

A matched pair
of angels.

CRIME SCENE

Before I even
make it back to the dressing area
I hear the commotion,
the shocked whispers
and someone saying,
What the hell?

I step in and see
a small blotch of red at my feet.
Another step and it flutters away.

The room is a crime scene,
swirls of red splashed across
the pale tiled floor.

The roses, my roses, stripped
of their petals,
stems broken and
                    thrown across the room,
petals,
        jagged
                    and ripped,
strewn everywhere.

Sofia and Mia arrive
and behind me, I hear Sofia's voice,
Who did this?

But I already know.

STAYING TALL

It is hard to stay TALL
locked in a bathroom stall
crying.

It's Kendall who raps
lightly.
Esme, you okay?

I can't respond.

I'm so sorry.
This sucks.

We're all sorry.

But we need to go.
It's time.

And I remember that
I have to dance.
Our contemporary number is coming up.

I sniff and blow my nose.
And open the door
to ten girls waiting.

You got this, Faith says.

Even Mia gives an
encouraging smile.

In the bathroom mirror
they get to work
fixing my face
wiping mascara from my cheeks
reapplying *Love That Red*
and smoothing my hair.

DESTRUCTION

But the aftermath of
destruction
is powerful, too.

On stage
we are distracted.
Mistrustful.

On the dance floor,
the Elite Twelve
are ravaged and ruined
and out of sync.

We are what is
left of us,
tattered petals
s
  p
   i
    n
     n
    i
   n
  g
        recklessly
                 without rhythm
                        without reason.

LIE

To save myself
from having to explain
     everything
I lie to Todd
     and Mom
          and Mrs. McPherson
about the roses.

When I meet them in the lobby
with my bags,
I tell them they were stolen.

I say how when we got back
from our performance
they were just
          gone.

And I don't mean to
but my eyes well
when I think about
the red fragments
scattered everywhere.

After the last routine,
we returned to the dressing
area to find someone
had swept the petals,
now cloudy with dust,
into a pile in the corner.

It's okay, Esme,
Todd rushes to say.
*It's okay. There'll
be lots more chances
for me to bring you roses.*

He pulls me into his arms,
and just like that
Todd has gathered the fragments
of me and made me whole again.

DOWN

At our next class,
Miss Regina comes in clapping
and we line up right away.
She's not happy with the team's
performance at the competition.

We run the contemporary number
over
        and over
                and over
                      again.

And still
she says
we don't look like a team.

We are off.
We lack cohesiveness.
She doesn't understand
      why.

When I push off
for my third grand jeté
I stumble
my foot tangled by something.

I crash
to the floor
      the palms of my hands
      and my torso
slamming hard.

The fall knocks the wind out of me
and I try to pull air back into my lungs.

In that moment
everything is quiet.
Even my panic
            feels silent
                no air, no noise.

Finally, my lungs
reset
and I take in a long breath.

Miss Regina is crouched
next to me
asking if I'm alright.

I nod
and she helps me to sit up.

I see Mia and Sofia
and Kendall and Faith
and the others
gathered around me
in a circle.

Brooke lingers in the back
taking a swig of her water.
She avoids my eyes,
which is the first thing
that is out of place.

When has she ever
missed an opportunity to
stare down at me in defeat?

Then Erin/Dimples says,
Miss Regina?
Esme was tripped.
Brooke did it.

Brooke's mouth opens in shock.

And then Flyer Reagan
speaks up. *I saw it, too.*
It was Brooke.

Miss Regina's face
darkens like a storm cloud
is passing overhead.

Brooke.
Outside NOW.
Bring your things.

AFTER A STORM

I am a downed tree
after a storm.
One minute I was up,
the next,
down.

I feel many arms around me
hands at my shoulders
and cupping my elbows
lifting me and walking with me
to the bench
where I am set down carefully
like a fragile thing,
a rose maybe.

Someone hands me my water.
Someone brings me an ice pack.
My palms still ring from
slamming down hard.
My chest, shoulders ache,
and my knee throbs against
the ice.

Damaged, sure,
but whole.

I think of Dad
going down
landing hard
with no one around
unable to get up
all day.

And I'm grateful
to not be alone
in the forest.

CROSSING A LINE

Kendall sits on one side
  of me,
    Faith on the other.

Mia and Sofia
   and the others circle around.

I lift the ice pack
and peek at the bruise already ripening
on my knee.

You alright?
Kendall asks.

I think so.

You know,
Kendall says
   to everyone
If Brooke did that to Esme,
she'd do it to any one of us.

She crossed a line.

I DON'T TELL MOM

about what happened during class.

When she notices me limping
I tell her I must've pushed too hard.

And when she asks
if I'm still up for going out,
I say, *I wouldn't miss it.*

THE "CLUB" IS NOT A CLUB

Not in the way that most people
think of a club.

It's not some city club
steamy and packed
with people wearing
tiny clothing
and smelling like
booze.

It's a community club
a plain building
with a parking lot in front,
looking more
shabby funeral parlor than
glitzy, neon nightclub.

Anyone can rent the space and
it's seen its share of
       retirement parties   bar mitzvahs   sweet sixteens.

But tonight it's a
Night of Music and Mayhem.
Three bands
(including Todd and Zoe's)
and open to anyone willing to pay
the $10 cover charge.

Mom pays the $20 for us to get in
and we're among the first to arrive.
Todd and Zoe and the rest of the band
are on the small stage doing sound checks.
Todd waves when he sees me.

A patch of empty dance floor
waits in front and
round tables scatter the sides of the room.
There's a bar in the back,
cast in shadowy lighting.

Todd looks great
in an Aerosmith T-shirt and jeans.
But Zoe looks amazing in leather pants
and a V-neck top
and big hoop earrings
that would make Grammy Jean proud.

Mom and I buy Cokes at the bar,
wave to Todd's parents,
and join their table.

Dad wanted to make it,
but after a long PT session
decided to stay home.

When I look around,
the place is starting to fill up.
I see a few other kids from school,
including Faith from Elite.

She calls me over
and I get up to say hello.
Turns out Christian, the bass player,
is her brother.

The lights dim and
we are on the dance floor
when the band plays its first song,
an old Mötley Crüe.

Faith and I dance.
Todd and the band play.

And Zoe,
Zoe was born
in leather
with a microphone in her hand.

WHAT MUSIC IS FOR

When the third song starts
I recognize the opening on the keyboard right away.

I tell Faith I'll be right back
and dash over to my mom.

Jim Croce?
She asks laughing.

But when I grab her hand
and tug her
toward the dance floor,
she says, *No way.*

Oh, come on, I tell her,
What is music for
if not to dance?

ON THE DANCE FLOOR

"Bad Bad Leroy Brown" has dragged
a lot of people
from their seats.

The floor fills with bobbing heads
and people singing the chorus
along with Zoe
about the baddest man in the whole damn town.

Mom bobs to the beat and laughs.
I want to remember this moment
for a long long time
so I pull out my phone
and grab a video to show Dad later.

When the song is over
everyone cheers.
Zoe thanks the crowd.

Mom pulls me in for a
quick hug.
They're amazing,
she whispers in my ear.
And then she heads back to the table.

I catch Todd's eye,
his smile so wide
I could curl up in it.

AT A SMALL BREAK

in the band's set
Faith and I go to get some water.

We stand in line
at the bar
and Faith talks about
how her brother Christian
is kind of in love
with Zoe, even though
he knows that
she's gay.

And I try to pay attention
as Faith talks,
but the entire time
some guy at the bar
is watching me.

STARING

He's clean-shaven,
college-aged, maybe older,
slick dark hair with
maybe too much product in it.

He spins his glass
on the bar top
while he stares at me.

Inside the glass,
amber liquid
licks against the sides.

He's with a friend,
a bearded guy, tall and thin.

His too-bold eyes
flick over me
from head to toe
and back again.

His stare lands and
lingers on my chest.

Most men
have the decency to
look away when
you catch them looking.

But this guy doesn't.

CROOKED

I keep my arms up by my chest,
holding my water,
keep myself TALL.

When he meets my eyes
he smiles,
a hitched smile, over
gleaming teeth
so crooked it shows
his pointy canine tooth
on that side.
Then he is getting up
and walking toward us.

HERE TO DANCE

Hello, ladies,
he says when he gets close enough.
How's it going?
Maybe he doesn't know
                    we're in high school.
Maybe he doesn't care.

He keeps his eyes on me
and smiles,
crooked again.
A dimple I didn't notice before
deepens at the corner of his mouth.

He gives off the kind of
cocky confidence you expect
from good-looking guys.

His friend stands next to him,
watching us like he's trying to
figure out how old we are.

Faith loops her arm through mine.
We're just here
to dance.

I noticed, he replies.
His eyes on me.

And if I was Little Red, I'd wrap
my riding cloak around my chest
and say to him
What big eyes you have . . .
Then Faith's arm tugs me
back toward the dance floor.

283

Have a good night, I say.

Yeah, you too, he says
and nods at me
looking like if I could fit in his glass
he'd drink me up.

CAN YOU BELIEVE THAT GUY?

Faith asks, as we wind our way
through the crowd
back to the dance floor.

It's getting more crowded,
but we find space.
Todd's eyes meet mine
for a hint of a beat
as he plays the opening
riff to
"Sweet Emotion."

His smile is sweet
and Faith and I cheer
and lose ourselves
in the music.

WOLF AT MY DOOR

When I turn
on the packed dance floor
my eyes catch slick dark hair
and too-bold eyes,
gleaming teeth.
The guy from the bar and his friend
are a few steps away.

I feel his eyes on me,
on my chest
again.
A sly wolf stalking his prey.

I turn away and move closer to the stage.
Todd, a few feet ahead of me
leans into his guitar,
losing himself in the music.

Then
in the blink of an eye
someone comes
too close behind me,
the sting of alcohol in my nose
        and the press of a body
                against mine.

Something brushes against my side

a hand with hungry fingers

that inch along

and then

cup

SQUEEZE

my breast.

I look over my shoulder
at gleaming teeth
and an ugly smirk
that seems to say
we share a secret now
before he turns away.

MOTIONLESS

Everyone around me
continues to dance
but I am dead wood
motionless in one spot
unable to move
unable to say
      or do
         anything.

When Faith dances my way again
she sees it in my face,
something wrong.

What is it?
she whisper-screams
over the music.

My eyes follow the Wolf
who laughs with his friend
as they walk
in the direction of the bar.

He swallows the last
of his drink.

I think he
just
      touched
           me—my breast.

As I say the words
in Faith's ear
my first thought is:
maybe I imagined it,
maybe my mind is playing tricks on me.

But no, I felt the fingers.
The squeeze.
That look he gave me.

Motionless now
on the dance floor,
the two of us watch the Wolf and his friend
as they walk to the door,
where the Wolf finds me
with his eyes,
and raises one corner of his mouth.

And then
he is gone.

WHAT HAPPENED

Mom stands up from the table
when she sees me
walking toward her with Faith.

What happened?

I don't know what to say
but I know I don't want to say
it here in front of Todd's parents.

Faith looks from me to my mom.

And then Mom tells
Mr. and Mrs. McPherson
that we'll be right back.

In the dimly lit hallway
outside the ladies room
Faith tries explaining,
There was this guy . . .

I add,
I think
　　　he touched my breast.

I draw in a deep breath
and hold in tears.

Mom holds my eyes
with hers and keeps her voice
steady.
Okay.
Is he still here?

290

No, he left, Faith says.

Okay, it's okay.
Well, it's not okay.
Mom's voice quakes,
But you're going to
be okay.

Mom wants to leave
but I want to stay
until Todd and Zoe are done.

Okay, we'll sit
at the table,
Mom says when she realizes I'm not giving in.

On our way
back to the table
Mom walks beside me
but places her hands on my shoulders
to steady me.

They remind me
of Dr. Lewis's hands on my shoulders,
her words,
Think TALL.

But in that moment
I can't do it.

I just want to shrink
to shrivel up
and disappear.

IN THE SHADOW OF NIGHT

Faith offers to stay with me,
but I tell her it's okay,
and she goes back to sit with her parents.

Mom and I wait at our table
for the last two songs of the set.

When they're done
Todd and Zoe make their way over.
Everyone is congratulating them
and when I say how good they were,
Todd notices that
something is wrong.

Let's get some air
he suggests.

Outside, the parking lot is
shrouded in shadow.
I scan for wolves.

When I'm sure the coast is clear
the three of us,
me   Todd   and Zoe
stand huddled
against the building.

I begin,
There was this guy

I say out loud,

He grabbed my breast.

What?! Zoe asks.

Todd looks into my eyes.
Maybe it's the shadowy night,
but Todd's eyes look like moss,
darker, deeper.

He asks if I'm okay.

I don't know.

TARGETS

And then Mom is there,
with our coats and her purse.

Todd and Zoe walk us to
the car.

And Todd leans into the passenger window,
I'll call you.

In the car ride home,
I slouch down in the seat.

Please don't tell Dad.

I don't know why
this is so important
to me, but it is.

Esme . . . are you sure?

Mom, please.

Okay,
but this isn't something you did.
None of this is your fault.

Mom's voice quakes
when she says,
No one has the right
to touch someone else
without their permission.

294

And in that moment
I can't help but think
this wouldn't have happened
if my boobs were smaller,
if I didn't have two huge
targets on my chest.

THE NEXT DAY GRAMMY JEAN CALLS

How are you doing, sweetheart?

Mom asked her to call
to check on me.

I don't know,
I answer.

I can't bring myself to say
how I really am:
      angry
              ashamed
                      embarrassed.

Listen to me,
Grammy Jean says,
*when something like this happens
you are going to feel A LOT of things.*

I'm quiet.

*But Esme, honey,
don't you go blaming yourself.*

*I'm just
so angry,* I say.
I don't say
the rest of it,
that I'm angry at myself.

I've replayed what happened,
over
       and
              over.

And every time I do,
I am angry at myself
    for being polite to the guy at the bar
    for thinking he was good looking
    and then for not screaming at the top of my lungs
    for not doing anything but standing there
                    helpless and embarrassed
    for not being on guard in the first place.

I should have screamed, I say,
or stomped on his foot
or kicked him in the balls.

Esme, honey,
you were in shock.

I shake my head
even though she can't see me.
It's just like you said,
about your friend with the orange,
I let embarrassment, politeness get in the way,

No, honey, Grammy says in a rush, *you didn't.*
You were in shock.
You let others help you.
There is strength in that, too.
You did the best you could.
Any woman, even the strongest of women,
would have reacted the same way.

Maybe, I finally say. *But, if anything like this*
ever happens again,

I'll scream and shout at the top of my lungs.

Yes, I believe you will,
she says.

And Grammy Jean adds,
Then kick him in the balls.

AT SCHOOL ON MONDAY

Faith finds me in the hall
and asks how I am.
I shrug. *Okay.*

She tells me quietly,
she is there for me
if I need anything.

I keep my head down,
my back hunched,
a stack of books clutched
like a shield
over my chest,
and go to my locker.

When I open it,
a note flutters out
and lands like a butterfly at my feet.

NOTE IN MY LOCKER

You mean
the world to me.

I am always
here for you.

     Love,
     T.M.

LEAN ON ME

And then he is there,
like by reading his note
I've summoned him.

Todd's hand reaches for mine.
Our pinkies loop first,
like they did on the armrest
at the movies.
Then the rest of our fingers
link together.

As we walk to class
I feel myself
leaning on him.

I hope he knows
if he ever needed it
he could lean on me, too.

It is the best
part of being in love,
holding each other up.

WHEN I GET TO CHEMISTRY

Celine takes one look at my face
and asks, in a voice
as quiet as I've ever heard from her,
Esme, are you okay?

And I tell her.
There next to the Bunsen burner,
and the rows of beakers,
while Mr. Silva walks to other tables,
I tell her.

And then she tells me
how one time, a football player
from another team
grabbed her ass.

*He pretended he didn't do it.
And I almost thought I imagined it.*

She shakes her head.
*But then he smiled at me
this jackass kind of smile
and that's when I knew
        he did it.*

Celine is quiet.
And then says   softly
I've never told anybody that.

        Really?

302

She shrugs.
I guess I was embarrassed
or maybe I thought
no one would believe me.

I'm sorry, I say.

I'm sorry for you, too, she says.

AFTER SCHOOL

In the band room
Todd plucks at his guitar,
but his mind is somewhere else.

He looks up every now and then
at me and Zoe, sitting in the back corner.

Zoe twists her hair
and says,

I'm just pissed.
I mean, what gives anyone the right?
I just want to find that asshole and smash his face in.
It's not right. It's just not right.

Zoe's eyes catch fire.
I'm so pissed.

Then her eyes soften.
Sorry, Esme, this probably
isn't helpful.

No, actually, I say, *it helps.*
Somehow it helps.

Todd sets down his guitar
and joins us.
And then I tell them about my visit
to Dr. Lewis.

Todd holds my hand
while I tell them about
my backaches and how hard
it is to dance.

304

I wouldn't blame you, Esme
Zoe says
if you decided to get the surgery.

Todd stays quiet,
and I can tell he doesn't want to
weigh in, like because he's male
maybe he shouldn't.

But Zoe doesn't let him
off the hook.
What do you think, Todd?

He looks from Zoe to me.

I don't know. It
seems   complicated. I hear you,
and your reasons for wanting to
make that change. But I guess—
I wouldn't want you to make that decision
because of
*   what happened.*
That doesn't seem right   you know?

And I think I do.

ABSENT

On Tuesday night, I tell Mom
I have a headache
and don't think I can go to dance class.

I haven't missed a single class
this season, but Mom doesn't push.

She just says it's fine
for me to stay home and rest.

We sit on the couch and watch
Finding Nemo
and I know we are both thinking
how the world is a dangerous place
full of dangerous things
Jellyfish, sharks
        or maybe wolves.

But also
there's a whole ocean
        of beautiful things, too.

        We just have to be
        brave enough to cross it.

ANOTHER LIFETIME

The bruise on my knee
is already turning
a mix of yellow and green.

The tripping incident
feels like
another lifetime.

Miss Regina leaves me a voicemail.
She says that she's been thinking about me
and looking forward to seeing me
so we can talk.

FEAR AND RAGE

It makes no sense
that some days
I am consumed by
    FEAR.

And some days
I am full of
    RAGE.

And I don't know
how to reconcile
these two emotions,
that run through me
like blue and red blood,
the same blood really,
one oxygenated, red like fire,
the other blue, like being frozen.

At some point
I'm guessing I'll have to choose
which path for the blood to follow.

Artery or vein . . .
RAGE or FEAR.

ALONE WITH MY RAGE ON WEDNESDAY

After missing last night's class,
I feel like I need to do something
to MOVE.

Alone, in the upstairs studio
on Wednesday, it is RAGE
that rushes through me
like a swarm of angry bees.

In my ears
the drone of a menacing buzz

powers my fury
down through my feet.

I stomp

        and STOMP

                    and STOMP
and JUMP

and THRASH—

My feet my legs   POUND
until
the twin targets
on my chest
heave
      and
            ache.

until
my heart
feels like it might
       burst out of my chest

until
my hair sticks to my temples
glued there by sweat
running down my face
my arms
my back.

Dr. Lewis was wrong.
I can't be TALL,
I can't pretend that cord is there
to pull me up.
Maybe I'll never see myself standing
TALL
ever again.

Because when I close my eyes
all I see is the leering look
of a wolf making small talk
and a smirk that sends a shiver through me.

RAGE is my fuel.
I flail
graceless
punching air and spinning out of control.

When I catch glimpses of myself
in the mirror
it is not pretty
and I do not care.

I am that swarm of angry bees
with no one to sting
when all I want is revenge.

If I can't sting,
how can I ever be free of this RAGE?

I dance and POUND,
through the pain,

until

my

strength

gives

out.

PUDDLE

I'm a puddle
on the studio floor.

All of my anger
my rage
my strength
maybe all of what makes me me
dripping
        pooling
                spilling away from me.

But
        maybe
                I get to choose
what I let go
and what stays.

I imagine the anger
the hurt
the shame
draining out of me,
leaking out of me,
like red blood
like the sweat
like the tears
that drip
dotting the floor.

I roll over onto my back
pluck out my earbuds
and close my eyes.

The cool of the floor
seeps into me.

My breathing evens out.

I know people have come back
from bigger tragedies than this.
But what if I have to deal
with this for the rest of my life?

There are no answers,
I know.
Big boobs or not,
surgery or not,
there is nothing
that guarantees
safety.

There is only me.

Only me
deciding what to let go of
and what to keep.

I let the cocky eyes and
the gleaming smirk
evaporate.

I replace them
with Zoe's fiery eyes instead,
I feel Todd's arms around me,
I hear Mom telling me to trust my heart,
Dad calling me Pumpkin from the dog chair,
Grammy Jean looking at me like I am a work of art

and her words,
What Would My Esme Do?

What would Esme do?

What will I do?

313

MAYBE

Maybe
I will stop hiding,
stop sinking inside my armadillo shell.

Maybe
if I keep these boobs
I should claim them.

They belong to me.
They are part of me.

Maybe
they are
not a burden to shoulder
not a trophy
not even part of a costume.

Maybe they can be something
other than twin targets on my chest.

If they are the first things
that people see when they see me,
and it seems like they always are,
maybe I should carry them with pride.

Maybe that
is the best revenge.

Maybe that is
what TALL
        is all
        about.

314

NEXT DANCE CLASS

I am quiet.
       Everyone is quiet.

Mia. Sofia. Kendall. Faith.
       All the others.
       But no Brooke.
Miss Regina comes in
and she's quiet, too.

She puts her hand on my arm
and asks how I am.

I nod and say *okay*.
She means the fall
but so much has happened
that she doesn't know about.

Miss Regina calls us around her
and then sits on the floor.
We sit, too,
crisscross applesauce.

Miss Regina tells us
that she appreciates
the girls speaking up
to let her know
what was happening
with the team.

315

No one, Miss Regina says,
should ever suffer in silence.
You are a team first.
You should take care
of one another.
Look out for each other.
Mia's eyes meet mine.
And then Faith's.
Kendall's.
All of us.
We look around
the circle
with fresh eyes.

Otherwise,
Miss Regina says,
the dancing
        doesn't mean anything.

THE ELITE ELEVEN

As we warm up, everyone starts to relax
like we're becoming ourselves again.

Like we can finally do
what we came to do.

DANCE.

Focusing on something
other than what happened
at the club
is the best thing for me.

We begin to
    reset
    regroup
    reblock
        the numbers now that we are down one.

Today, dancing feels familiar
and new at the same time.

I don't worry about
my chest. Let my new bras
do their job, so I can do mine.

I pull myself
TALL.

At the break
Faith joins me
asking quietly
    Doing okay?

Better, I say.   *This helps.*

Kendall and Abbey and Reagan and Erin come over.
The whole dynamic is different, isn't it?
Kendall asks.
I nod.
And Erin says,
I don't think I realized
how much she was weighing us down.

And then Mia and Sofia
and the others
join us.
Sofia asks, *Esme, have you been*
working on your
double stag?

I shrug. *A little.*

Looks good, Sofia says.

Yeah, really great height, Mia adds.
She smiles
and I know she means it.

I show them
the stretches I found on YouTube.
And then we're talking
                              laughing
                              the way I always pictured Elite.

Miss Regina
stands back, pretending to
look over something on a clipboard
but I catch her smiling.

318

DAD PICKS ME UP

from dance class
because Mom is working.

How was class?

Good, I answer, and I mean it.

On the drive home,
an awkwardness settles around us.
Finally, I feel brave enough
to ask, *Did Mom tell you?*

He glances over at me,
and I can tell he knows.

It's okay, I say.
I don't blame her.

Are you okay, Pumpkin?

I think about what Miss Regina said. *No one should suffer in silence.*

And I tell Dad
about how I'm angry,
so angry about what happened
and how sometimes I'm just scared,
like if this could happen,
what else might happen.

We park in the driveway and talk.

And he says he feels like that, too,
so angry and also a little scared
because I'm growing up
and he can't protect me like he used to.

But your mom and I,
we're always, always
going to be here for you.

which reminds me
I've always had a team.

THE PHILOSOPHY OF MOM

In my basement studio
practicing my turns,
I hear Mom come
down the stairs,
and I take out my earbuds.

In the space next to the water heater
she has rows of little sproutlings
popping up from seeds
under hanging grow lights.

Next month she'll
transplant them
in the garden outside.

Oh, hi, Esme.
Sorry, I didn't know you were down here.
I'll be done in just a minute.

But I don't want her to go.

I come and stand beside her,
as she pours water into the trays
under the pots,
adjusts the fluorescent lights.

How are the plants doing?

Mom hides her surprise.
I've never asked
about her plants before.
Good. I think it's going
to be a good crop this year.

And I know she's remembering
the failed garden last summer,
how she worked so many extra hours waiting tables
the garden dried up and got choked by weeds.

It's a lot of work, huh?
All these little seeds in pots,
I ask.

She puts her arm
around me.

Yes, but it's the best kind of work,
caring for something.

Even when you don't know
all the millions of ways
it can all go wrong.

Storms.
Disease.
Disaster.

That's life.

But you can't think about that.
You just have to trust
they'll make it.

You plant them,
care for them
talk to them
love them
and then
love them

some
more.

And then Mom
plants a kiss
on top of my head.

ON HER WAY UP THE STAIRS

Mom turns around
and calls to me
from two steps up.

I stand at the bottom
looking up at her.

I was thinking,
she says,
maybe it would be good
for you to
talk to someone,
you know,
about what happened.

She waits for me
to answer,
gripping the railing.

That might be good, I answer.

HOW TO SAVE MYSELF

I've been thinking
about what Grammy Jean
said, about aerobics
and how it saved her
when Grampa Tom died.

And I think
I understand now.

When I dance
I'm reminded
of who I am
that I am strong.

I feel a strange kind of power
run through me,
like I can stand TALL again.

But maybe talking to someone—
a counselor, a therapist—
would help, too.

Maybe through dance
and talking about it
I can free myself of
RAGE
and stop being all
FEAR and claws.

Maybe doing both
is how
I save myself.

BETTER OFF

The next day
I walk to the studio as
a light drizzle leaves
teeny dewdrops on my fleece.
The air smells like
the world is waking up.

I pass the elementary school,
looking forward to the quiet
of the studio.

Hey, Esme!
I turn and see Brooke rushing toward me,
Jane a few steps behind,
empty swings still swinging behind them.

Adrenaline kicks off
in my chest.

Brooke stands in front of me,
and without hesitation,
fires off what I'm sure she's been waiting to say:

Hey, thanks for getting me kicked off the team.
No, really. I was all done with that group.

She waits like I'm going to respond.
I don't.

The rain is coming
harder now.
Colder.
The sky growing darker.

326

Jane stands to the side,
watching us.

Brooke keeps going:
I don't know what Miss Regina was thinking.
You never belonged on that team.
You're not good enough.

The bees buzz in my head.
FEAR or RAGE
What will it be?

Then Brooke says,
You'll never be good enough.
Especially with those huge boobs
throwing you off balance.
She shoots me a cruel smile
a gleaming smirk
a jackass kind of smile.

Something in me tightens
at the sight of it.
I find my words.

You crossed the line, Brooke.
You got
EXACTLY
what you
deserved.
And the team
is better off without you.

For a second,
I think she's going to hit me.
I almost want her to.

Give me that outright assault,
one that leaves a mark,
instead of one hidden,
delivered in secret, without
a bruise or blood to show for it.

But then Jane
steps
            between
                        us.

ENOUGH

Jane says.
Enough.

She turns to Brooke and grips both her shoulders.

Come on. Jane's voice is steady.
That's enough.

And Jane steers her friend
away from me.

I'm left behind,
drenched in the rain,
watching them walk away.

EPIPHANY

Alone in the upstairs studio
I dry myself off with my sweatshirt
careful to mop
up the rain I've tracked across
the floor.

The surge of adrenaline
I felt outside melts away
as I move slowly.

I am easy with myself.

This place has become a refuge
a place for me to think
and find my way back to myself.

For a blink
I hear Brooke's voice
HOW GOOD COULD YOU BE?

And I realize
       maybe
              I've been hearing the question WRONG
                this whole time.

HOW GOOD COULD YOU BE

HOW GOOD COULD YOU BE

  if you just
     ignored the voices in your head
       trusted in your body
         kept yourself TALL
           and danced from the heart?

THE STUDIO FLOOR

I arrive twenty minutes early
before Thursday's class
to practice alone again
in the upstairs studio.

I move lightly
dance and step easily
shaking loose any doubts.

When I press my torso
to the cool of the studio floor
my nose touches down and
I breathe in
       the smell of
       sweat and body lotion and Lysol
            and laughter and tears and music and joy.

This is what love smells like, too.

CONVERSATION I OVERHEAR #5

When I'm done,
I am halfway down the stairs
when I hear Miss Regina's voice,
Girls, what is this about?

I tuck myself against the wall
out of sight.

Miss Regina,
Kendall's voice says
with all the confidence that is
Rebel K,
*We think you should give Esme
Brooke's solo in the lyrical number.*

Miss Regina's voice has an edge to it.
You know I make my own decisions.

Triple Threat Catie rushes in to say,
We know. But we want you to know what we think.

Esme's the best choice,
Faith, the Nice One, says.

Have you seen her lately?
Erin with Dimples adds.

Yeah, she's amazing,
Sofia the Soul Star says.

There's a lot of chatter that follows,
girls in agreement.

Then Small But Powerful Mia
slices the air with her voice,
No one works harder than Esme.

Miss Regina says,
Well, you might be right about that.

DANCE COMPETITION #3

IN THE LOBBY

I see Mia's parents.
Mia's mom spies me and rushes over
trotting in her heels,
her bracelets clacking.

She opens her arms to me
and I step inside them.

Esme, honey,
we got your note,
she whispers.

And Mia's dad
smiles with his perfect
dentist's teeth,
No thanks needed, kiddo. We're glad to help.

And all I manage to say
(again) is *Thank you.*

Then I spy Mia
coming out of the dressing area.
When she sees her mom
pull me in for another hug,
Mia smiles.

DEAR SPOTLIGHT

Please
    be
        kind.

Here I am
    draped in chiffon,
    the color of a summer sky,
    ready to fly
    in a solo
    that I've claimed as my own.

The crowd
    out there
    my parents
    Todd and his parents
    in the dark
    hushed in this moment
    before I begin.

I promise, Spotlight, to   let your light
    lift me and to
    forget the world's eyes
    and just dance.

Dear Spotlight,
    Catch me.
    Lighten me.
    Set me free.

MY HEART RISES

from the cavity
of my chest
and lodges in my throat.

But I don't have to speak.
I will let my body
be my voice.

Once the music starts
I forget the spotlight
forget the eyes
forget the judgment.

We dance as a team
and I am center of the universe
at least for a moment.

HOW GOOD COULD YOU BE?

Here,
let me show you.

BECOMING

I become
free
fearless
flying
over the expanse of the stage,
wide as the sky.

I become
light like feathers
lifting off, catching wind

G L I D E

I R
C C
E L

d
i
p

CAREEN

E
S
I
R

I become the strength in me.
I become the lyrics of the song.
I become the music all around.

I even become
the applause.

338

MORE THAN DANCE

After,
Mia finds me
in the dressing area.

That was beautiful, Esme.

It's an origami sentence.
Apology and love and forgiveness
folded in tidy creases.

Thank you, Mia.

She nods and looks like she
wants to say something else.

We used to tell each other
everything
and now
we have forgotten
how to talk at all

I wait. Finally
she says, *I just wanted to tell you
that I'm not doing Elite
next year.*

*I'm changing studios.
Sofia and I—
we're going to Teague's
to focus on pointe.*

I nod and manage to say,
*Well, that makes sense.
You're amazing at ballet.*

She turns to go.
Mia?

When she turns around
I see four-year-old Mia
grinning at me
as we race to the tape line.

I'll miss you, I say.

Yeah, me too.

And we both know
we mean
more than dance.

HOLDING SPACE AGAIN

Maybe
      probably
things will never be the same with us.

I never imagined
a time I couldn't talk
      to Mia.

I also never imagined
how many others would
take up residence in my heart:
      Todd
      Zoe
      Faith
      Kendall
      even Celine.

But I know
no matter what
my heart will
always
hold a space
for Mia.

THE PHILOSOPHY OF ESME

The world is full of
pinheads and
wolves and
people who think
they can
        grab you
        jab you
        trip you.

They want you to fall.

But if that is true,
this is also true:
        The world is full of love.

        Of all kinds.

        The love of a grandmother
        who sees you as perfect

        The love of a dad
        who wants more for you than he had

        Of a mom
        who cares for you, shelters you, watches you grow

        Of friends
        who use their voices for you when you can't

        Of a first love
        who holds you up and treats you like something to be cherished

I see now
how all those loves
braid together,
to form a strong, steady cord
that runs through my center,
like the axis of the earth.

I feel it when I dance,
a pull like gravity
no longer my nemesis,
keeping me centered.
I let it curve and spin and slide
with me.

Becoming my spine
a strong central line,
my true north.

I find the cord, feel it
pulling me upright
pulling me TALL
pushing me forward
pushing me up
       up
           up
               until
       I am
SOARING.

ACKNOWLEDGMENTS

This is not the first novel I've written, but it's the first one to be published. It's been a long journey, but through all the ups and downs, I've always been incredibly lucky to have the unwavering support of the people in my life.

Starting with my parents, who were not readers themselves, but who raised a reader by taking me to the library, letting me pick my own books, giving me crumpled dollar bills to spend at school book fairs, and allowing me the luxury of talking about the stories I read and later about the stories I wrote.

When I was in high school, my mum brought the stories I wrote to the restaurant where she worked as a baker and showed them to everyone. (I'm sure the waitresses, cooks, and dishwashers were all thrilled to read the ramblings of some random ninth-grader.) The year before she died from cancer, she gave me a homemade birthday card, a simple folded piece of white paper, *Sweet Sixteen* in her curlicue cursive on the front. Inside, she penned the most hopeful, most sincere wish for me about becoming a writer and how she knew it would happen. Even now, whenever I read my stories aloud, I always hope my words find a way to her.

And my dad, who, when I published a short story in a national literary magazine for high schoolers, surprised me with a brown padded desk chair, a Brother word processor with a three-inch screen, and a desk so big he had to cut a foot off the back with his circular saw just to fit it in my tiny bedroom. Still, I know what it meant that he bought all the accoutrements he imagined a budding writer would need, all on his machinist's salary with money that I'm sure was needed elsewhere.

Special thanks to my older brothers Mike and Gary Nickerson, who

I think never understood why I loved to read or loved to write, but who cheered and supported me anyway.

For my other parents for the last thirty-plus years, my in-laws, Fred and Noreen DeChambeau, thank you for—everything.

Thank you to those teachers who believed in me and supported me as a writer, especially in my last year of high school, when Mum had died and college applications were due: Mr. Patrick Cronin, Mr. Paul Dunphy, and especially, Mr. George C. McCabe.

To my longtime friend and boss at the VA, Bill Warfield, thank you for appreciating this creative side of me, for giving me time off when I needed it, and for encouraging me to pursue my writing even when we were deliriously busy at work.

Thank you to Grub Street and to the New England Society of Children's Book Writers and Illustrators and to all the kindhearted writers I've met there along the way. Thanks as well to Bethany Hegedus and her Courage to Create crew and the Writing Barn.

For my WCYA peeps at Vermont College of Fine Arts, I am so grateful that I found you when I did. Thank you Tom Birdseye, Jane Kurtz, Linda Urban, and Nova Ren Suma, for your wisdom, support, and encouragement! Special thanks to Libby Wheeler and all my dear Wrights of the Round Table—I love you all! This story bloomed during a VCFA Workshop, the crocus of my heart pushing through the Vermont snow of that winter residency. It was the first time I'd written in verse, and I had twenty pages under the tentative title *Boobs*. Under the wise leadership of Cory McCarthy and Louise Hawes, the amazing and generous writers of our magical workshop convinced me that there was something worthwhile in the story and the way it was being told. Special thanks to: Mitu Malhotra, Tamera Breckenridge, Ali Borger-Germann, Drew Chilton, Nicole Crail, Erin Nuttall, Jenifer Pillock, Lauren Riley, and Anne-Marie Strohman.

For the Associates of the Boston Public Library, a million thankyous! I'm not sure this story would have found its way in the world had it not been for your generous support and the gift of being named the Associates of the Boston Public Library Writer-in-Residence. Jennifer DeLeon, Elaine Dimopoulos, Desmond Hall, Alan Andres, and

Meredith Goldstein, thank you for your support and encouragement and for answering all of my questions during that glorious Residency year (and beyond)!

Thank you to Amy Francis and Tina Geniuch for your friendship and for answering my dance-related questions!

Hugest thank-you to my wise and all-knowing agent, Elizabeth Bennett, and the team at Transatlantic Literary Agency, for seeing the promise in Esme's story. Elizabeth, I am so grateful for all your patient guidance and for seeking me out and meeting me at the BPL.

Sally Morgridge, my wise and patient editor, thank you for seeing all those things I couldn't see for myself in the text of this story. I've loved our exchange of ideas, and this book is so much better for it. For the whole team at Holiday House, thank you for making me feel so welcomed and supported. For the bold and brilliant cover art, big thank-you to artist Ana Ariane!

My husband Chris never stopped believing that I'd be published. When I told him I wanted to go to grad school to get my MFA, spending time and money, both of which always seemed in short supply, he said simply: *You should do it.* And: *We'll make it work.* With every rejection, he stood at my side, with a ready hug and the unreasonable confidence I needed, saying, *Don't worry. It will happen. I know.*

For my kids, Donna and Colin, who, from the time they were little, have watched me write, trying (and most times, failing) not to interrupt me. I love that you've been on this journey with me, as I squeezed in writing time in the evenings and on weekends and on my days off, when I sometimes dressed in work clothes (to keep up appearances) and shipped you off to school so I could secretly have the house to myself to write. I hope you are lucky enough to find what you love to do and you do it, even if you do it on the edges of everything else, and whether or not you make a living at it.

Finally, Chris, Donna, and Colin, I dedicated this first one to you because I know you will recognize yourselves in these pages. The three of you will be part of every story I tell, the way you will always be part of me.